*To Daisy and Rocky—
two swell cats!*

Contents

1
The End of the Rope

ome on, Abbey. You can't sit down!"

The group of teenagers straggling through the depths of the jungle were completely exhausted. One of the young men reached down, seized the blonde girl by the arm, and pulled her to her feet. "They've almost caught up with us!" he gasped. "We've got to keep going!"

"I can't go any farther!"

"You've *got* to, Abbey," the boy said firmly. "They're only a few minutes behind."

The speaker was tall and gangly, with auburn hair and blue eyes. His name was Josh Adams, and he was the leader. He looked around quickly and saw that Sarah Collingwood was not in much better shape than Abigail Roberts.

Sarah, however, had her lips drawn up in a determined line. She took Abigail by the other arm. "I'll help you, Abbey," she said. "We can't stop here."

The other four members of the group, all young men, looked to be as bad off as these three.

Dave Cooper, at fifteen, was tall, athletic, and handsome, but now his clothes hung on him in rags, and his cheeks were hollow.

Jake Garfield was a slim redhead. His clothes also were ragged, and he was huffing and puffing. "Don't know if we can make it this time!" he gasped.

Another fifteen-year-old, with light blue eyes and pale bleached hair and wearing a cowboy hat, looked in better shape than the others. He was breathing hard, but there was still a natural strength in him, and he said quickly, "Maybe I should go back and head them off."

Josh managed to grin at him. The boy's clothes were in tatters, but the hat looked good. "No, let's stick together, Reb," Josh said. "I know you're ready to fight a sack of wildcats, but we don't have anything to fight with. Let's just get going."

"Are you all right, Wash?" Reb turned to a small black boy, the youngest of the group at thirteen. He was sitting on the ground, drawing in deep gulps of air.

"Yep, I'm all right," he said, getting up. "But my feet won't go any faster." He looked over his shoulder and shivered. "I heard a fellow say once, 'If you hear a footstep behind you, don't look back, 'cause something might be gaining on you.'"

Josh slapped the boy on the arm. "I guess that's right. And it's hard not to look back when something's after you."

He'd no sooner spoken than Abbey slumped down again and put her head in her arms. She began sobbing without control, and the others looked at her helplessly.

Sarah Collingwood leaned over and patted her shoulder. "We're all right. We've been in worse spots than this, Abbey."

"No, we haven't! We've been running for days now. Every day we've almost got caught. We're all going to die!"

Her hysteria was almost infectious, Josh saw. Everybody, weak from lack of food and sleep, was in bad shape. He thought, *If I were just a good leader, I'd know what to do. But we've run so hard and long, it looks like the Sanhedrin's going to get us this time.*

As he stood there despairing, wondering when the soldiers of the Sanhedrin would come bursting out of the jungle, he thought about how far he and his friends had come since being brought to this strange place called Nu-world.

All seven of them had been hidden in sleep capsules on planet Earth, just before a nuclear war. Years had rolled by, changing almost everything, including the geography of the earth and the beings that inhabited it. And they came out of the sleep capsules to find that the world was in a struggle between good and evil. The evil was led by a strange being called the Dark Lord. His henchmen were a council called the Sanhedrin. They were a powerful force and were filled with hatred for a good leader called Goél.

At the thought of Goél, Josh said as heartily as he could, "We'll get out of this. Goél won't let us down." He sincerely hoped this was true.

He knew Goél was gathering his forces in Nuworld for a battle against the Dark Lord and the Sanhedrin. Goél had already sent the Seven Sleepers to several places to help Goél's people. Now, as they were returning from one of their missions, they had been ambushed by the Dark Lord's soldiers. For days they had struggled through this thick jungle, and now it looked as if they were not only lost but doomed.

Wash was watching Josh's face. "It don't look too good, does it?"

Reb slapped Wash on the back. The two had become fast friends, though they had not liked each other at first. "Why, sure, we'll get out of this. I remember the many times General Robert E. Lee got penned up and looked like he'd lose, but he'd come out of it."

Jake stared at the tall cowboy with a sour expression. "He lost the war though, didn't he?"

Reb didn't like to be reminded that the South had not won the Civil War. He glared at Jake. "Well, we ain't los-ing this one. I think—"

"Be quiet, Reb! I hear something." Josh held up a hand with alarm.

Instantly Abbey stopped crying and sat up. As they all listened hard, she said under her breath, "We're going to die—I just know it!"

"We'll fight 'em with whatever we've got." Reb pulled a pocketknife out of his tattered trouser pocket, opened it, and looked into the jungle defiantly. "They're getting close, I reckon. I can hear them."

Someone was indeed coming through the jungle, and it could only be an enemy.

"Get ready," Josh said. "We'll do the best we can. You girls head on out of here. We'll hold them off. Maybe you can get away."

"No, we're all staying together." Sarah's blue eyes flashed as she faced the wall of green jungle. "There," she whispered. "There they are. They're coming!"

Forms moved out of the greenery, and Josh, who had been ready to see the red cloaks of the soldiers of the Sanhedrin, yelled, "Look! It's Mat and Tam! And Volka too!"

The two approaching in front were short—not much more than three feet tall. They were fat as sausages. Their bellies gave promise of exploding any minute and were held in by broad, black leather belts with shiny brass buckles. Both had plump red cheeks and small black eyes peering out from under bushy brows. Both had beards that came almost down to their belt buckles. The newcomers looked identical.

"Well, I knew I'd have to come and get you out of a mess sooner or later!" one of them declared crossly.

Grinning, Josh said, "I know you're Mat. Still the eternal pessimist." He shook the dwarf's hand and turned to his exact replica. "And you're Tam. I know you've got a good word."

10

Tam grinned broadly. "Why, we'll get out of this. It's just a piece of cake."

Mat and Tam had been with the Sleepers on their first adventure. They were Gemini twins, looking exactly alike but the exact opposite in spirit. Whereas Mat was grumpy and always seeing the dark side of things, Tam was jolly and always cheerful.

Tam turned now to the third newcomer and said, "We've got your old friend here. You remember Volka, don't you?"

Volka was no less than a giant. He was enormous, towering over the Sleepers, twice their height. He had huge bulging muscles and a rather simple face. "Ho!" He beamed. "It's me!"

At once he was surrounded by Sleepers pulling at him. They'd always liked Volka.

Sarah said, "Now I feel safe with you around."

Mat scowled. "Well, you're *not* safe. The Sanhedrin troops will be here in five minutes."

"What're we going to do?" Abbey wailed. "I just can't go any farther."

"Why, don't worry about that." Tam grinned. "Pick her up, Volka." He watched the giant reach down and do so. "Now," Tam said, "come this way. We'll show you something you'll like."

The Gemini twins turned and plunged into the jungle, and the Sleepers followed. Volka brought up the rear, carrying Abigail, speaking to her from time to time, but she appeared too worried to answer.

They made their way down a trail, and though they were exhausted, the Sleepers were so cheered by the sight of old friends that everyone seemed to gain new strength.

"How did you know to come after us?" Jake asked.

Tam looked back and grinned. "Why, Goél sent us to get you."

"Is he close by?" Wash asked hopefully.

"Not far," Tam answered.

"Far enough that we need to hurry up. If you'll stop dragging your feet," Mat complained.

The Sleepers moved as quickly as they could. The rain-forest trail was very narrow, and the trees were so tall that little sunlight filtered down below. The jungle floor was almost bare here because small plants could not grow due to the lack of sun.

After they had crossed two small streams, Tam directed them to walk through the trees to their left for a hundred yards. "This probably won't throw them off our trail completely," he said, "but it's the best I can do. Come along."

Soon the forest began to grow less dense, and finally when they were all practically falling down, Tam said cheerfully, "Look, there it is!"

Josh, right behind him, looked up to see a house with a steep thatched roof. A half dozen strange-looking figures stood in front of it. His heart leaped up.

"I'm so glad to be away from the Sanhedrin!" Sarah said.

Abbey raised her head from Volka's shoulder and looked. "Why, it's just an old house!" she exclaimed. "Surely Goél won't be *there*."

"Any port in a storm," Dave Cooper said. "As long as they've got something to eat and some clothes for us to put on, I'll be happy."

They walked into the clearing, and indeed the house was very old. It was built of small logs.

One of the odd-looking people came forward—a shaggy-haired man, his garments made of black fur. "You found them," he said in a deep voice.

"Yes, Zohar," Tam said. He turned to the Sleepers and said, "This is Zohar. He is our leader. And Zohar, these are the Seven Sleepers you've heard about."

He named them off, and the strong-looking man's gray eyes gave each one almost a physical touch.

Zohar nodded when Tam had finished and said, "You are tired and hungry. We will eat, then we will talk."

"I say amen to that," Wash said. He looked at Reb and winked. "I wish they had some hominy grits and hog jowl, don't you, Reb?"

Reb grinned faintly. "I bet you'd settle for moon pie and Dr Pepper, wouldn't you?"

Wash nodded. "I sure would. Seems like the things I miss most from the old time is moon pies and Dr Peppers."

The Sleepers threw themselves down to rest while some of the inhabitants began cooking over an open fire. They were strange-looking people indeed. Some were tall and thin and pale, others short and muscular, not much larger than Tam and Mat. The nuclear explosion had done strange things to the inhabitants of Earth, so that these human descendants looked little like people from the time of the Sleepers.

Yet they seemed to be loyal and good, so the Sleepers relaxed. They sat around sipping the delicious liquid that one of Zohar's helpers had produced, and soon the meal was ready.

When the seasoned meat was put before them, Reb opened up his knife and began slicing it. "Where's Goél?" he asked. He stuffed a huge piece of meat in his mouth and chewed furiously. "Boy, that's good!" He closed his eyes and chewed even faster. "What is this anyhow?"

"Wild pig," Zohar said. "We had good hunting this morning."

"If I just had some barbecue sauce to put on it," Reb said, "it'd be perfect. But is Goél here?"

13

Zohar looked around and shrugged. "He was, but he had to leave."

"When will he be back?" Josh asked.

"He not say," Zohar grunted. He seemed to be a man of few words, and Josh could get nothing more out of him for the time being.

Looking around her, Sarah saw another house down the way. Other people were moving about it, and some of them finally came to greet the Sleepers. They were mostly wounded men, some of them terribly so. There were also women and children. All looked tired and frightened.

After the meal was over, Zohar sent the people away and sat down to talk. "Goél says that you should rest until he sends for you."

Abigail was looking up at the rather dilapidated house. It seemed ready to fall in. "I'd hoped we'd get something better than *this*," she whispered to Sarah. "It looks awful."

Sarah did not complain, however, and soon the two girls were shown their sleeping quarters.

Zohar led them into the house and pointed to a ladder, then upward. "You sleep there." He nodded at a woman, who gave them two rather thin blankets, and then the girls climbed to the dim loft, where they found some straw and nothing more.

At once Sarah began to fix a bed for herself. "I'm so tired, I could sleep on stone."

She lay down and watched Abbey try to fix her hair.

They had lost all their baggage, and now the blonde girl's hair was stringy and her face was dirty. Her mouth was turned down in a sour look, and she said, "I'll never get clean again. And look at my hair—it's awful!"

"Well, we all look pretty awful, but we'll get cleaned up tomorrow. I'll fix your hair for you, and we'll find something to wear."

14

Abigail gave her hair a yank, then plopped down on her blanket. Pulling half of it over her, she began to complain again. "What good does it do, Sarah?"

"What good does what do?"

"All that we've been doing for Goél. We've been here for over a year, living with cave people, living under the ocean, living with bird people. And we've helped all of them—but the war isn't any closer to being over."

"Goél sent us on those missions. If we hadn't gone," Sarah said, "these people would all have been lost to the Dark Lord."

"But we can't go *everywhere*. You've seen the Dark Lord's soldiers—there are thousands of them. They have weapons. What do we have?"

Sarah was almost asleep, but she heard Abbey's question. She turned toward her and said gently, "We have Goél." It disturbed her that Abbey was so bitter.

She had known for a long time that Abbey was spoiled. *And if I was as pretty as she is,* she thought, *I'd have been spoiled too.* But now she saw that there was resentment in the girl. "You've got to learn to look on the inside of things, Abbey. Not the outside."

"What does that mean?"

"Well, no matter how bad things look—circumstances, I mean—there's always hope." She tried hard to think of an example and said, "Remember the American Revolution at Valley Forge? The Americans were starving and freezing, and the British had so many trained troops with all the weapons they needed and food. If anybody looked at that, they would've said, 'Those Americans will never win their independence.' It just looked hopeless."

Abigail looked over at her friend, and there was rebellion in her smooth face. "That doesn't have anything to do with us," she muttered.

Sarah reached over and patted Abbey's hand. "Yes, it does. Washington and his army were in a hopeless situation—but they won. And we'll win too. You'll see."

Abbey stared at her unbelievingly. "I'm going to see if I can go to sleep. This blanket's probably got fleas in it."

2

The Rebellion of Abbey

I'm worried about Abbey." Sarah looked over to where Josh was struggling to repair one of his shoes.

"I'm worried about all of us," he said. "Look at this!" He held up the tattered shoe and shook his head. "It's falling to pieces."

Sarah held up the blue shirt she was mending. A large rent had been made in it, and she had borrowed needle and thread from one of the women to sew it up. "Well, what about this? All of our clothes are worn out. But that's not what's bothering me most."

Josh picked up an awl and punched a hole in the thin leather. Then he took a piece of rawhide and shoved it through the hole. Making a knot, he said, "This will have to do, I guess. We've got to be shod if we're going to do very much." He glanced at her. "I know what you mean about Abbey."

"She's not very strong. And she's not as tough as the rest of us."

"That's right. And besides," Josh said, "she's worried about her looks all the time."

"She can't help that, I suppose."

"*You* help it," Josh countered. "Why, with a big glob of dirt on your face, you don't even care. Think what a fit Abbey would have."

"Dirt! Where's dirt?" Sarah groped in the small bag at her feet for a piece of mirror. She stared into it, then glared at the boy, who was laughing at her. "You're a beast, Josh! Just a beast!"

"I guess I look like one." Josh ran a hand through his long hair. "We all need haircuts and baths and clothes—just about everything."

The two sat talking, and finally Sarah asked, "Do you ever miss things back in Oldworld?"

"Sure I do. But we can't go back, so we'll have to make the best of things here."

Sarah stared at him, thinking how Josh had matured so much. "Well, you're right. We've talked about that too many times, I guess. But about Abbey—she's just not . . . not mentally ready for these hardships. She's too soft and genteel."

"Well, she's had a year to get toughened up. I don't know what else to do for her." Suddenly he looked up. "Look, there comes Zohar. He's kind of a mean-looking character, isn't he?"

"Yes, but I'm sort of glad for that. It feels good to have a strong man like him around. Hello, Zohar," she said when he got closer. "Did you come to help us with our sewing?"

Zohar had little sense of humor. "No," he said. He stood over them and was indeed formidable-looking. He was dressed in a ragged bearskin, tied with a wide leather belt around his middle. Inside the belt was tucked a wicked looking battle-ax with a razor edge. He stared at them for a moment, then said, "We go."

Sarah and Josh looked at each other. "Go? Go where?"

"Goél sends message. We go there." He pointed toward the north. "We go soon. Tomorrow."

"What did the message say?"

"It say, 'Some of the House of Goél need help.' We go help."

"We're not in very good shape to help anybody," Josh said. "We're not even able to help ourselves much. Did

Goél say that everybody was to go? What about your women and children and the wounded?"

"They stay. Strong men go." He put his hard, dark eyes on them and nodded firmly. "Goél say all Seven Sleepers go to help those in the House. We leave early."

As he walked away, Josh said, "You know, every time he walks I expect to feel the earth shake."

"Abigail's not going to like this. I don't like it much myself."

"Neither do I. But if Goél ordered it, then we've got to go. I'll tell you what—I'll let you break the news to Abbey, and I'll tell the rest of them."

Sarah found Abigail in the loft trying to brush her hair.

As soon as she spoke of their new mission, Abbey's eyes flashed. "I'm not going!" she said. "And that's final."

"But you've got to go, Abbey. We all do."

"No, we don't. Anybody with half sense knows we wouldn't be of help to anyone. Why, we're half-starved— we don't have decent shoes—and look at this awful thing I'm wearing." She held out her knee-length tunic. It had been well made and still had a little color left in it, but many washings and mendings had rendered it decidedly sad-looking. "I wouldn't be seen *dead* in this thing!"

"It won't matter. We're all in the same shape." Sarah began to grow irritable. Abbey was a sweet girl, but her moods got on Sarah's nerves. *For some reason she thinks she's better than the rest of us,* she thought. "You'll *have* to go, Abbey."

"I'm not going. You can tell Josh and that awful Zohar that I'll wait till they get back."

Sarah stared at the petulant girl, then shrugged and climbed back down the ladder. She went to find Josh and report Abbey's response.

19

"Why, she's *got* to go!" Josh snapped. "That's all there is to it."

"I think the only way she'll go is if you tie her and have Volka carry her. She won't go under her own power."

"Well, we'll just have to convince her." Josh's face was grim, and he went off to have a confrontation with Abbey.

When he came back, he was scowling. It appeared he had had no more success than Sarah. "We've got to leave in the morning. Try to talk to her again, Sarah."

But nothing availed, and the next day when the Sleepers prepared to march out with Mat, Tam, Volka, and the Nuworld warriors, there were only six of them.

"It seems a little bit funny with only six of us," Reb said doubtfully.

"Are you sure you tried everything, Josh?" Dave asked. "I don't like to see us split up like this."

"I don't like it either, but that's the way it is."

At that moment Zohar called out, "We go."

And the Sleepers trooped off. They all felt disturbed at leaving Abbey behind.

Abbey was watching from the loft window, and as the troop disappeared down the trail, she had a sudden impulse. She turned and started toward the door, thinking, *I've got to go with them. I can't stay here by myself.* But then, stubbornly, she stopped and shook her head. "No," she said aloud. "I'm not going. You have to draw the line somewhere."

She dressed and climbed down the ladder carefully. A few people were up and stirring, and Zohar's wife offered her some breakfast. It was a thin gruel and some sort of leftover meat.

Abbey shook her head. "No, thanks."

She stepped out into the open air and for a time wandered around the camp. More than once as she walked she had the impulse to run and join her friends. *It's not too late*, she thought, and she struggled between two desires.

But finally she said, "I'll rest up and maybe find myself something nicer to wear and maybe find some good soap. I'll be ready to go on the next mission."

She felt better after convincing herself of this and walked toward the stream that wound its way through the forest a quarter mile from the house. The brook was clear and bubbled merrily over the rocks. From time to time, she picked up a stone and threw it in. And more than one frog leaped off the banks with a croak of alarm.

She wandered farther than she'd planned and was about to turn back. But first she knelt at the water and washed her face, enjoying the coolness of it. "I wish I had some soap," she said aloud. "I'd give anything for a hot bath and to wash my hair."

"You should have it, my lady."

Abbey leaped up, startled by the voice. She turned to see a tall young man wearing a sky blue suit of some shiny material.

He pulled a hat with an eagle's feather in it off his head. His hair was long and black and fell over his shoulders. He smiled at her, his teeth very white.

"Who are you?" she demanded.

"My name is Lothar. I have come a long way."

"What do you want?" Abbey was more impressed with his looks than she cared to admit. *He is handsome!* she thought. *And look at that diamond on his right hand. I've never seen such a large one.*

The man called Lothar put on his hat, looked around, and then glanced back at Abbey. "I seek a group called the Seven Sleepers. Do you know of them?"

Abbey was startled but said, "Yes, I know of them. Why do you seek them?"

"That," Lothar said politely, "I can only reveal to the Sleepers themselves. Can you direct me to where they are?"

Abbey hesitated. She had grown cautious in Nuworld, as had all the Sleepers. Strangers were not to be trusted until proven. But surely this one was safe. She took a deep breath and made her decision.

"I am one of the Sleepers," she said. "I am Abbey."

The dark eyes of Lothar fixed on her, and he smiled again. "Well, I am fortunate. Can you take me to your friends?"

"They're gone on a mission."

Disappointment swept over Lothar's face. "That I regret," he said. "Will they return soon?"

"They shouldn't be gone too long."

He stood and thought, as if he had forgotten her. "Well, that presents a problem."

As he pondered, Abbey studied his fine garments and noted that he was not only splendid-looking but was also strong and athletic. Finally she said, "Perhaps if you'll tell me what you want, I can help."

"Maybe so. In any case, I have no choice." He hesitated only a moment more, then said, "I come from the Empress of the Underworld. You have heard of the Kingdom of the Underworld?"

"Why, no, I don't think I have."

Amazement flashed across Lothar's handsome features. "I'm shocked to hear it. Your education's been neglected!"

"Is it far from here?"

"A two-day ride. Are you sure you have not heard of our Empress and her wondrous kingdom?"

"No, never."

"That will make things even more difficult. I have a message here for you." He pulled a parchment from the inner pocket of his tunic. "Are you the leader of the Sleepers?"

"No, Josh Adams is our leader."

"Ah, but he is not here. Still, you may read the message and give it to him."

Abbey took the letter and opened it. It said, in beautiful script:

To: The Seven Sleepers

We have heard of your courage and willingness to serve those who are fighting against the Dark Lord. I, the Empress of the Underworld, beg you to come and help us. We are in great danger. We send the heir to our throne, Prince Lothar, with this message. He will accompany you back should you choose to come.

Empress Fareena
Ruler of the Mighty Kingdom of the Underworld

Abbey looked up at the tall young man. "We have gone on missions like this before. But, of course, what the Empress asks is impossible just now. When the others come back, we may be able to do something."

"Could not you come and explain that to our queen?"

"Oh, no. I couldn't do that."

"Why not? It would be very simple for you to leave a letter for this . . . Josh."

But Abbey could only shake her head. "No, it must not be."

"That is a regret to me."

"Can't you wait one night? Perhaps they'll make a quick journey."

Lothar seemed to think about her request and nodded. "I could do that." He looked at her oddly then. "You would like my country, the Underworld."

Abbey wrinkled her nose slightly. "It sounds awful—like living in a hole in the ground."

Lothar laughed aloud. He was very good-looking when he laughed. "You would not say so if you were to come with me." He held up his hand with the huge diamond and asked, "Do you see this beautiful stone?"

"Yes. I've never seen one that large."

"Large? Why, I've often been criticized for wearing such a *small* stone. In our throne room the walls are lined with stones like this. Also red and green and purple stones, more beautiful than anything you've seen."

"Oh, it sounds beautiful! Not at all like a hole in the ground."

"A hole in the ground? No, indeed." He began to describe the underworld kingdom, mentioning that they had learned to spin beautiful silk and satin cloth.

And the thought of the women's gowns in yellow, red, pink, and gold made Abbey's eyes glow.

"We've learned to make good food too. Let me offer you some of this." He opened the bag that was slung over his shoulder. "Come and sit. While you eat, I will tell you more about my world."

Abbey sat down and began to sample the food. It was delicious! Better than anything she'd ever had. She said so.

"Why, this is just trail food. At one of our banquets you would taste something really good. Here—drink some of this."

Abbey took the small silver flask that he offered, tasted the drink, and said, "Oh, it's delicious. What is it?"

"Just something we make for the royal table. I'm glad you like it."

The food made Abbey's eyes brighter. She drew her

knees up and said, "Tell me more about your country, Prince Lothar."

"Oh, you must not call me that. Lothar is fine. And perhaps I may call you Abbey?"

"Oh, yes, please do."

She sat and listened, while the prince leaned back and talked. His country sounded like a fairy-tale land the way he spoke of it.

Then his face grew dark. "But we're in danger. Terrible danger."

"Danger of what?" Abbey asked.

"We may lose our kingdom to the Underlings."

"The Underlings? Who are *they?*"

"They are a terrible race who inhabit part of our kingdom. They're cruel and fierce." His voice shook with anger. "And they would kill us all if they could."

"How awful!"

"Yes, it is. They've already killed my father."

"Oh, Lothar. I'm sorry."

He shrugged and said, "They've tried to kill me many times. So far I've evaded them, but they grow stronger. Even while I'm away, I'm afraid they will strike at the queen. Then they will take the throne, and we will all be killed. Those beasts would rule our beautiful kingdom."

"Tell me about the empress."

"Ah, you would love her. She is beautiful and has many powers. Yet she is only one, and she has asked that you come. She has never asked for help before, so I fear the situation is perilous."

He talked for a long time, finally saying, "Will you not come with me, Abbey?" His voice was gentle, and he took her hand. "It would be a wonderful sight for you, and you would be a jewel in my kingdom with proper clothes and your hair done as only my people know how to do it. Besides, you would be doing a great service for the House of Goél."

Abbey hesitated, then shook her head. "I can't decide now."

"Very well." He released her hand and got to his feet. "I can wait until morning, then I must return."

"I will find you a place to stay tonight. But it won't be what you're used to," she warned.

"No, I will remain in the forest. I would rather not be seen by anyone tonight. I will wait here, right at this spot. At dawn tomorrow, if you're not here, I will have to leave without you." He shook his head. "What a shame if you do not get to see the land of diamonds and rubies!"

As Abbey walked back to the old house, she longed to visit the beautiful kingdom that Lothar had described.

That night she slept poorly. She knew that she would have to make a decision—and somehow she knew she would *have* to at least see a country where diamonds lined the walls!

3
Another Visitor

Abbey was awakened very early. A yellow beam of sunlight came in through the window and fell full on her upturned face. She gave a start and a sharp cry. Her eyes flew open, and she sat up, calling in alarm, "Who is it?"

Then after looking around rather wildly, she laughed. "I'm as nervous as I've ever been in my life."

She threw back the blanket, rose, and dressed. Going down the ladder, she saw women busy cooking some sort of grain for breakfast.

It was flat and tasteless, and she could not eat it. Remembering the delicious food that Lothar had produced, she thought, *What a shame to have to eat this stuff when they're eating so well in the Underworld!*

Outside, the sun was shining brightly, and she walked down the trail to where the small stream gurgled over rounded stones and into a quiet pool. Quickly she washed her face in the cool water and took out a brush and tried to do something with her hair. *It's so dirty*, she thought again. *I wish I had some good shampoo or soap.*

The only soap she had been able to find had been coarse gray lumps that had burned her hands. It was so strong that she was afraid it would make her hair fall out.

After she had done the best she could with her hair, she leaned over and looked at her reflection in the water. The pool was still, and she studied her face carefully. She had a heart-shaped face, lips gently rounded, and very large blue eyes.

"I wish I had some lotion," she said aloud. She touched her face, thinking, *I'm going to have rhinoceros hide if I don't do something.*

Finally Abbey rose and made her way slowly along the creek. She still did not see Lothar. Perhaps he had gone for a walk. Several birds sang in the trees, strange-looking birds of a bright orange color that she didn't recognize. They had beautiful voices, though. They harmonized almost as if they were members of a choir.

Abbey stopped and looked up, listening with admiration. She loved music and was herself a fine singer. She had even played the piano at one time. But there were no pianos that she could find in Nuworld.

All of a sudden she gave a start, for someone stepped out of the undergrowth and was walking toward her along the trail that led beside the bank.

He was a rough-looking young man, not much older than herself, shabbily dressed and very dirty. His hair hung down around his shoulders. It would've been probably auburn if it had been clean. He was pale, and his eyes were staring at her.

"Who are you? What do you want?" Abigail called out with alarm.

"I'm looking for the Seven Sleepers."

It occurred to Abbey that perhaps this was a friend of Lothar's, yet they hardly looked to be of the same class. This young man was perhaps as tall as Lothar, but he was clothed in rags. As he came closer, she saw that he was even dirtier than she had thought. Dirt was caked in his hair, around his fingernails—his hands, she could see, were worn with hard work. And his gray tunic was stiff with grime. He was barefoot, and his feet were bruised and caked with mud. And then she saw that he had very intense gray eyes.

"I've come a long way," he said. "My name is Beren." He looked hungry and nervous.

Even as he spoke, something made a sound in the woods, and he turned quickly, pulling a knife from his belt and holding it out in a guarding position.

Abbey wished she had not come so far from the house. A few men were there, but even if she cried out they would not be able to reach her in time. She decided to act with as much assurance as she could.

"My name is Abigail," she said. "What do you seek of the Sleepers?"

"I come from a far country," he said wearily. He slipped the knife back into his belt, turned, and held out his hands. "Can you direct me to the Sleepers? I must find them."

Abigail hesitated. *What if he's one of the enemy—an Underling? He looks like a thug. I'd better not tell him I'm a Sleeper.*

"They've gone on a mission," she said. "I think they won't be back."

The young man named Beren seemed to sag. He shut his mouth in a thin line and shook his head. "I *must* find them. Where have they gone?"

Abbey pointed in a direction quite the opposite from that which the party had taken. "They went that way. There's a lot of them. A big band—all armed," she lied. *That ought to discourage him,* she thought.

Beren stepped closer, and she drew back in fright. "Don't you touch me," she said.

"I haven't come to harm you, but I must—"

At that instant, Lothar rounded the bend in the trail that followed the brook. When he saw the stranger, he let out a cry and drew a bright sword. He ran toward them, calling out in a language she did not understand.

Beren wheeled and ran down the creekside.

29

Lothar came up to Abigail and stopped. "I could never catch him. He's too fast. Did he harm you?"

"No, he didn't harm me. But who is he?"

Lothar replaced the gleaming sword in its sheath. "He's one of the Underlings." He pulled off his feathered cap. His hair was very black and gleamed as the sunlight hit it. It was thick and full and fell down over his neck. "One of the enemies of the lords of the Underworld and the rightful people of that land."

"He looked awful!"

Lothar laughed. "If you saw the others, you wouldn't say so. What was his name? Did he tell you?"

"He said he was Beren."

"Yes, I've heard of him. Well, lucky thing I came along." He stepped closer and took Abbey by the arm. "I think we'd better go to the house where you are staying. We'll be a little safer there."

"Safe from what? He didn't look like he could harm you."

"He may not be alone, and some of the Underlings are quite monstrous. Huge beasts with evil eyes and totally merciless. They'd cut your throat without a second thought."

"Yes, then maybe we'd better go to the house."

As they walked back, she said, "He came looking for the Seven Sleepers. What do you suppose he wants with us?"

"Why, to kill you, of course. They're the enemies of Goél and all that he stands for. They've killed many of our own faithful servants."

"How awful!"

"Oh, yes. They killed my own father, remember." Pain came into Lothar's eyes, and he lowered his head. "I don't like to think about that. But if something isn't done, I may be the next to go."

"Lothar, how truly awful! That mustn't happen."

The tall youth turned to her. His face was very serious. He put his hand out, and she placed hers in it trustingly.

"I hope that it will not, but we've fallen on evil times. Our empress does all she can. She has mighty powers, but there are many Underlings. No matter how many we capture, it seems there are always more. They're as clever and wicked as any being in Nuworld."

"What do they want?" Abbey asked.

"As I said, they want to kill the empress and all the nobility. They want to take over all the riches of the Underworld. They serve the Dark Lord. He promised them all sorts of things if they would come under his banner."

Abbey said nothing for a while. At last she said, "That sounds like an old story. Ever since we came to Nuworld, Goél has sent us to people in trouble like your own."

"Yes, we have heard much of that. We have heard the song about the Seven Sleepers." He looked down at her and smiled. "It still seems passing strange to me that so much could rest upon such a beautiful young woman, so tender and gentle. Like a princess."

Abbey flushed. His praise sounded sweet in her ears, but she said modestly, "I'm the least of the Sleepers."

"Nevertheless, to be a Sleeper is an honor, isn't it?"

"Oh, yes, it is." Abigail could not help thinking that only yesterday she had been complaining about being a Sleeper. But somehow this handsome young man, with his winning ways, had softened her.

Lothar was quiet for a time. But when they came in view of the house, he put a hand on her arm. "Stay a moment."

When she faced him, he asked quietly, "Have you made your decision? Will you go back with me and help save my people from the Underlings?"

"Oh, Lothar. I don't know. It's so hard to choose."

He did not urge her further. "Yes, it must be," he said. "That shows you have character. Why, most young women, if they had the opportunity to go to the Underworld and have all the jewels, silks, and other beautiful things there—they wouldn't hesitate a moment."

"Oh, I'd love to go, but I'm not sure it would be the right thing to do."

"You must decide." Lothar shrugged. "You must come voluntarily or not at all. But you must make your decision now. I must hurry back. Even now the Underlings may be in revolt and the empress's life in danger."

Abbey's mind seemed to go into some sort of frenzy. More than anything else in the world, she wanted to go with Lothar. The very idea of the gold, jewels, and luxuries he had drawn for her made her want this. On the other hand, something kept nagging at her—a doubt that she could not set aside.

She said, "I just can't make up my mind, Lothar. I wish I could. If I had my own way, I'd go in a minute."

Lothar shrugged again. "Well, perhaps it's not important that you go. Are there other young women in your party?"

"Yes, there's one. Her name is Sarah."

"It might actually be better if she went instead of you."

Abbey turned to look at him. "Why her instead of me?"

Lothar smiled. "She cannot be as beautiful as you."

Again Abbey's face glowed, but she asked, "What does that have to do with it? Is it better for a homely girl to go instead of a pretty one?"

"Why, surely you've heard of the powers of our empress?"

"No, I told you—I've heard nothing about the Underworld."

Lothar laughed. "Everyone knows about the power of the Empress of the Underworld to make women beautiful."

Instantly Abigail's total attention was riveted on Lothar. "To make women beautiful, you say?"

"Why, yes. Of course, you are already beautiful. And this other girl, this Sarah, if she goes—I hate to tell you this, but after the empress touches her with the strange power she has—" he shook his head "—she'll be far more beautiful than you, I'm afraid."

Abbey thought, *That's not fair!* She stared at Lothar and said, "How does she do this?"

"It's not for me to explain the powers of the Empress of the Underworld. But that would be true for any girl who goes with me. For this Sarah, if she will come."

Abbey was like a person who had come to a fork in the road. On one hand lay the dangers, bad food, and lack of clothing that she had known with the Sleepers. On the other road lay the wonders that Lothar had described for her. She thought longingly of the luxury and the ease.

Then an image of Sarah popped into her mind, clothed in silks, satins, jewels, and more beautiful than herself! And a voice whispered, *Maybe it's the thing to do. Maybe somehow it's all working out that you will go before the others do.*

As if he'd heard her thoughts, Lothar said, "You know, it's possible that you might go with me to look over our problem. You could get some decent clothes and some rest. We have hot springs there that make a lovely bath and all sorts of soaps—things that girls like. If you don't like it—" he shrugged "—I can always bring you back."

"I'll do it," Abbey said. Suddenly going with Lothar

seemed the very thing to do. "I'll leave a note for my friends, and then I'll be ready to go."

"Very well. I'll just wait at the creek for you. Can you ride?"

"Yes. I'm an excellent rider. Why?"

"Because I came here on horseback, and I brought a beautiful mare—just for you, I see now, although I didn't know it at the time."

"I'll hurry as quick as I can," Abbey promised. She ran back to the little house.

In a dither, she found paper, wrote a note, and gave it to Zohar's wife. "Give this to Zohar or to Josh when they get back, will you?" She scarcely waited for the woman's nod before turning and running down the pathway.

When she arrived at the creek, she found Lothar waiting with two beautiful horses. Both were black as night.

One was smaller than the other, and Lothar said, "This is Star. She will be your horse. She's very gentle but fast as the wind. Quickly now!"

He helped her into the saddle, then swung on the back of the larger horse and turned to smile at her. "And now we will go to the magnificent Kingdom of the Underworld. Soon you will be dressed like a princess."

4
Kingdom
of the Underworld

It was fortunate for Abbey that she'd had much experience in riding. Before coming to Nuworld, she'd never sat on a horse, not even a pony. However, her adventures with the Sleepers had required this means of transportation. She had fallen many times but through persistence had learned to be almost as good a rider as Sarah.

She sat now upon the black mare and followed Lothar down a narrow path, which twisted through the rain forest. The cries of strange birds came to her ears above the soft padding of the horses' hooves. The floor of the forest was soft, carpeted with what seemed to be hundreds of years of pine needles. They had been traveling hard since dawn, stopping only once at noon to rest the horses for an hour and eat a meal. Now Abbey was weary but was determined not to complain.

Just as the sun dropped behind a line of trees, Lothar pulled his large steed to a halt and looked around. "There's a stream right over there." He pointed to his left, then glanced at her. "I expect you're tired. We'll stop there for the night."

"I can go on further," Abbey said stoutly.

"No, it'll be dark soon. We'll make a fire and cook a meal."

Lothar led her to a slight rise. "This will stay reasonably dry, even if it rains." He slipped off his horse, then held a hand out for her.

She took it, dismounted, and he smiled.

"You're a fine rider," he said. "There aren't too many of those among my people."

"I've had a lot of experience," Abbey said.

"I'll gather some firewood, and you look through these supplies and see if you can find something good to cook." He tied the horses, while Abbey prowled through the large saddlebags. By the time Lothar had a fire going, she could say, "We're going to have a fine supper. I'll show you what a good cook I am."

"Good," he said. "And I brought a small tent for you to sleep in. I'll make you a bed of pine boughs. It won't be as good as the apartments in the palace, but you'll have some privacy."

As Abbey began to fry meat in a small pan, she watched him remove from a saddlebag a dark blue tent that seemed to be made of fine silk. He cut poles and stakes with a sharp knife, and she was delighted when he turned and waved at the small shelter.

"It's beautiful," she said. "I wouldn't mind having a dress made out of that material."

"Its color would go with your eyes." Lothar smiled. He came over and sat down. "Is supper about ready?"

"Yes. I've done the best I could." She put the meat and bread before him. He had brought along two delightful, collapsible silver cups. She opened them, admired them, and filled them with sparkling spring water. "No Dr Pepper tonight, I'm afraid."

"Doctor who?" Lothar asked in surprise. "We don't have a doctor here."

"Oh, that's just the name of a drink we used to have back where I lived."

Abbey found the tender meat to be very good. Lothar approved of it too. Then she opened a package and said, "I don't know who made these, but they're delicious."

They were small cakes, sweet and mouth-watering. "What's in them?"

"Honey, I think. I'm no cook. I'm mostly an eater."

The two of them finished eating, then sat back and watched the fire as it crackled merrily.

"Tell me more about the Kingdom of the Underworld," she said.

Apparently nothing could have pleased Lothar more. For an hour he talked about his home. "You would never know, by walking over the ground, what is underneath," he said. "There are compartments filled with gold and precious metals. There are huge caverns where we store food of all kinds—mostly wild grain. We have our own mill by an underground river. You'll like the underground river. It goes to a rocky channel, and the stones are so bright they're like lamps lit up. They reflect on the water. I'll take you for a boat ride when we get there."

"And you make all the things you need to live underground?"

"Oh, most everything." Lothar shrugged. "It's like other kingdoms in some ways."

"How's that, Lothar?"

"Well, we have different classes of people." He went on to describe the structure of the Underworld. "At the top, of course, is the Royal Family, which is now the empress and myself. Then we have our nobles. You'll be meeting all of them. The young nobles will all fall in love with you and want to marry you."

He laughed at her blush. "I didn't know girls knew how to blush. You'll be the belle of the ball. I can see you now, wearing a beautiful new red dress with diamonds and a crown on your head and boots made out of finely tanned moleskin and ruby rings on your fingers and an amethyst necklace . . ."

He went on and on, and Abbey enjoyed it hugely.

"I wish we were there," she said excitedly. "I'm so anxious to meet the empress and all the nobles. But there are other people who do the work, aren't there?"

"Oh, yes. We have our mercantile class—that is, people who work for a living. They make things, buy things, sell things—I don't know most of them too well." He hesitated, then said, "Of course, in a kingdom like ours it takes a lot of work. We're continually expanding— digging new tunnels, creating new storerooms and new underground villages."

"Who does all that work?"

"Well, when an Underling is captured, we make him do that work. We make slaves of them, of course."

Abbey's face fell. "I don't like to think of people being slaves."

"It's their own fault," Lothar said. "They'd kill us in a minute if they could. We have to keep them in chains, or they'd ruin the kingdom." He looked over at her and said, "You're sleepy, I think. We have one more day's hard ride. Good night, Abigail. I'll see you in the morning."

Abbey went into the little tent and was delighted to find that he had made a bed of soft pine boughs covered with smooth blankets. She rolled into them and soon went to sleep, dreaming of a palace with beautiful ladies and handsome men twirling around in a ballroom.

"Well, it's been a hard ride, but we're finally here." Lothar motioned toward a steel gate set in a sheer wall of solid rock. It was a large gate—big enough to admit two wagons side by side. It had no windows and seemed to be fixed.

"It looks so big," Abbey said in surprise. "How do you get through it? I don't see any hinges."

Lothar laughed. "That's the idea of this gate. You can't get in. Only a few of us know the combination."

Abbey looked at him with surprise. "I don't see anything to turn. Safes have knobs, don't they?"

"Not this one. It has a spell on it."

"A spell? You mean, like magic?"

"Something like that." Lothar smiled at her. "It'll open only for the words that are known to very few. Stand here now, and I'll show you."

Abbey watched as Lothar advanced to within a few feet of the gate. He looked up and began to chant in a language she didn't understand. It gave her an eerie feeling, for his voice sounded odd—not like Lothar's voice at all. When he finished, he gave a cry and said, "Look! The gate opens."

Inside was a passage made of solid rock. It sloped downward ever so gently, and the walls were lit by glowing stones. She moved her horse closer to one side and touched them. They glowed with a pale green light, and she muttered, "It's like indirect lighting."

"What? Oh, yes, I suppose so. We don't have to carry torches in here," he remarked. "It was the work of many generations to gather these stones and set them in place."

"It's beautiful," Abbey said.

The floor was stone, and the hooves of the horses rang on it. The road went on and on but never grew narrower. The echo of their voices rang in her ears.

"What's that ahead?" she asked, pointing.

"It's a guard post," Lothar said. "See those armed men? It would take some stout fellows to get past them."

He pulled up his horse as a man wearing a black cape and steel helmet came forward. He was very pale, and his eyes studied them carefully. "Welcome back, Prince Lothar," he said in a deep voice. "We've all been waiting for you."

Lothar nodded. "I have a guest, as you see."

The guard bowed low and stepped to one side. "Admit Prince Lothar and his guest."

The guards that had drawn up in a rank moved back. All held spears with tips that glittered coldly and wore swords at their sides. The shields they carried on their left arms bore a curious device that Abbey had never seen. "What is that emblem on that shield?"

"Oh, that is the emblem of our empress. Rather beautiful, don't you think?"

Abbey said, "It's a little frightening. I never did like snakes much."

"Most girls don't." Lothar laughed. "But it's the emblem of our kingdom."

They rode past the first guard point and afterward passed others.

"I would get lost in here. It twists and turns so much."

"Part of that's on purpose," Lothar said. "This is our first line of defense. No army could come in here with huge forces—they'd have to come in small groups to fit in the tunnels. And we have made certain that they would not get far. Let me show you something else."

He rode forward for a few feet, pulled his horse over to one side, and then said, "Now, do not come any closer." He waited until Abbey reined in her horse, then reached out and touched a spot on the wall.

Instantly, the road fell away in front of him.

Abbey gasped as she saw a dark, cavernous hole where there had been what seemed to be solid rock.

"I would not advise you to fall into that hole," Lothar said. "There are things at the bottom that would make quick work of you." He laughed and touched the wall again.

The road, which was apparently on hinges, swung slowly back into place.

"Now, we can ride over it," he said.

Abbey was nervous as she urged her horse over the trap, for she heard the snapping of sharp teeth and huge jaws down below.

"That's just one thing we discourage our enemies with. But come along."

After what seemed a long journey, they turned a corner in the tunnel, and Abbey gasped.

Prince Lothar turned to look at her with a smile. "Beautiful, isn't it? People never forget their first sight of the palace."

"It's—it's more beautiful than anything I've ever seen!"

The palace that she looked on was made, it seemed, of crystal. It rose up out of a huge underground cavern with lights flashing and glimmering from the points of the crystals. Overhead, stalactites hung down, also reflecting light. The floor itself seemed to be glowing. The palace, like something out of the Middle Ages, was composed of turrets that rose majestically almost to the top of the huge cavern. They were, she saw, large crystal walls that enclosed the lower parts of the palace.

"Come," Lothar said. "You'll have time to admire it later. The inside, I think, is more beautiful."

He led her through walls that seemed made of a mixture of rock and crystal. Here the guards were dressed more ornately. Plumes floated from their steel helmets. "These are the empress's guards," Lothar said. "They are the personal bodyguards of the Royal Family."

Abbey followed him till they came to a smaller building, where servants came at once to take their horses. She patted her mare on the nose and said, "You're a fine horse, Star. I hope I see you again."

"Well, you will, of course. She will be your personal horse as long as you're our guest." Lothar took Abbey's arm and led her along a glowing wall until they came to a magnificent double door. The guards saluted, and he nodded as he muttered a password to them.

When inside, Abbey was once again shocked. Here was much glimmering light from the glowing stones. Lanterns burned, throwing their light down over the magnificent entryway. She saw statues that must have taken years to carve, and everywhere glittering stones were set. Some of them formed beautiful pictures.

"Follow me. I will take you to your attendant."

"My attendant?"

"Yes, your personal maid while you are with us."

Lothar led her down a series of halls and finally entered a smaller room, where they found an older woman. "Luna, this is your mistress, Mistress Abigail. This is Luna, Abbey. She'll be your servant."

"How are you, Luna?"

Luna was a small woman with white hair. She was very pale and rather frail. She came at once and curtsied deeply.

"I am your servant, Miss Abigail."

"I'll leave her to your charge," Lothar said. "See that she's well dressed for her audience with the empress."

"I'm going before the empress?" Abbey asked anxiously.

"Oh, yes. You'll have dinner with us tonight. I'll see you then. Perhaps you might take a little rest." He halted, turned, and took her hands. He lifted one of them and kissed it, saying, "I'm glad you've come to be part of our kingdom, Abbey." Then he left the room with a quick step.

"If you'll come with me, I'll show you to your quarters," Luna said. She led the bewildered girl farther down the corridor and turned into a doorway that was made from a light wood Abbey had never seen.

Inside, she looked around with delight. A huge bed with pink silk coverings was in the middle of the room. It was obviously an overstuffed bed, and she longed to throw herself onto it and sink into it. Then she was busy looking at the pictures that lined the walls, all done by an expert hand. And at the furniture, which was more elaborately carved than any she had ever seen before.

Luna said, "Perhaps you'd be interested in a bath, my lady?"

"A bath? Oh, that sounds wonderful."

"If you'll come this way, I'll assist you."

Abbey stepped through a door, and her eyes grew large. "I've never seen a bathroom like this." She was looking at a tub that was at least eight feet in diameter. Steam rose from it, and it was made of glowing, pure white marble. "How do you heat the water?" she asked.

"It comes from a natural hot spring. It is very relaxing. You'll find soaps and lotions. I'll wash your hair as soon as you bathe."

For the next hour, Abigail soaped, lathered, rinsed, and floated on top of the deliciously fragrant water, for Luna had added a scent to it. She found something like bubble bath and poured it in liberally, so that soon bubbles covered the top of water and overflowed onto the floor. Then she lay back and Luna washed her hair carefully.

Finally, wearing a beautiful nightdress, she sat in a silken stuffed chair as Luna dried her hair with soft cloth and brushed it till it gleamed.

"That feels so good!" Abbey whispered, her eyes half closed.

"If you would like to lie down and rest, I think you'd be much more refreshed."

"I think I will." The bath had made her sleepy. When Luna turned the covers back, she sank down into what seemed to be an enormous feather bed. "Oh," she whispered, "this is wonderful!" She went to sleep instantly.

She had several quick flashing dreams, but when she woke forgot them at once.

"It is time for you to dress for the audience with the empress, my lady," Luna said.

Abbey sprang out of bed and stared at the soft undergarments that Luna had laid out. They felt smooth next to her skin, and she thought, *A lot better than the feed sacks I've been wearing lately.* Then she turned and saw The Dress. "Oh, my," she said in a whisper. "I never saw such a dress!"

It was a dress not often seen. It seemed to be white, but even as Luna turned it, green, blue, and red sparkles flashed from it. She looked closer and saw that tiny jewels woven into the material created the sparkles.

She slipped into the dress, and Luna fastened up the back. When Abbey turned to look in the mirror, her lips opened with delight.

"You're beautiful, my lady," Luna said. "Very beautiful. Let me get your jewelry." She led Abbey over to a chest on the top of a fine side table and opened it.

The glitter of precious stones, gold, and silver made Abigail blink. For a long time, she tried on necklaces and rings. Finally she settled for a tiara of what seemed to be huge rubies to decorate her head, and a bracelet of diamonds with a large green stone that glittered under the light.

"I think you're ready now," Luna said.

At that moment, a knock came at the door.

When Luna opened it, the prince stood there. He was clothed in white with scarlet trim on his uniform. Gold buttons adorned it, and he looked more like a prince than anyone she'd ever seen.

He smiled. "You look beautiful!" He came in and took her hand. "Let me take you to the Empress of the Underworld."

5
Empress
of the Underworld

As Abbey entered the magnificent banquet room, its glittering beauty made her catch her breath. The ceiling was very high, giving the impression of enormous size. The walls were elaborately carved, showing scenes of, she supposed, the history of the Underworld. There were battles and scenes of empresses and kings in state, all carefully carved into the solid greenish rock.

Suspended from the ceiling were immense chandeliers. Tiny candles burned in them like miniature diamonds. Their light flickered over the room below, and as Lothar led her forward, she saw that the tables were filled with richly dressed men in uniform and women wearing beautifully colored dresses. She felt every eye on her.

"I'm a little nervous, Prince Lothar."

"Don't be," he said cheerfully. "Just hold my arm. Come now, and we'll introduce you to the empress."

"What do I call her?"

"Her name is Fareena. You can call her simply Empress."

On a raised platform was a table covered with a white cloth. On it golden dishes and silver utensils gleamed, and in the exact center of the platform sat a woman such as Abbey had never seen.

"This is Empress Fareena, ruler and master of the Underworld," Lothar said. "And this, My Empress, is Abbey. She has graciously consented to be our guest."

Empress Fareena was a beautiful woman with pale skin, jet black hair, and the most penetrating green eyes that could be imagined. She wore a scarlet gown and a huge diamond solitaire on her right hand that winked and flashed with each movement. Her dress was low cut, and a glowing green stone hung from around her neck. It was intricately engraved with the sign of a serpent, Abbey saw, on its surface. Remembering herself, she curtsied low and said, "I'm honored to be here, Empress Fareena."

"Come closer and let me look at you, my child." The empress watched the girl approach and smiled. "You have chosen a beautiful representative, Prince Lothar."

"Yes, I do have good taste, don't I?"

The empress smiled again, then said, "Be seated. We are ready to begin the banquet."

Lothar escorted Abbey to one end of the table, seated her, then walked around and sat across from her.

As soon as they were seated, the empress said, "We did not have time to have a full company, but such as we have, you are welcome to, my dear Abbey."

"Oh, I can't imagine anything more welcoming than this."

"You like our kingdom, do you?"

"I've never seen anything like it," Abbey said, her eyes glowing. "I was all wrong—I thought that any kingdom underground would be dirty and ugly, but this is beautiful."

"I'm glad you find it so," the empress said with satisfaction. "The prince has told you something of our history?"

"Yes, a little, but there's much I don't know."

"Then we will inform you, but first we will eat."

Immediately a procession of servants, all of them pale and undersized—and looking very thin and hungry—began to file by, carrying silver and golden vessels. The sadness of their faces was in violent contrast with the setting.

46

These must be the Underlings, the slaves, Abbey thought.

None of them smiled, and they kept their heads lowered.

When a younger servant dropped a fork, the empress hissed at him. "You fool! Be careful!"

The Underling began to tremble and mutter his apologies.

"You'll find yourself back in the mines if you don't watch what you're doing," Empress Fareena snapped. Then she turned back and smiled. "They're hard to train, the Underlings, for service like this. They're good for nothing but digging. But let me ask you about yourself, my dear Abbey. Tell me how you came to this place. We have heard of the Sleepers but of course have never heard the truth. I think the truth is important, don't you?"

"Oh, yes, Your Majesty. Very important."

"Good! We are agreed then. Tell me the story of the Sleepers."

Abbey spoke freely of how the Sleepers had come to Nuworld. She became so engrossed in her tale that she forgot to eat, but there was always an Underling there to give her hot food. She told of their adventures and how Goél delivered them from death not once but many times.

"Ah, yes, Goél. A mighty, mighty power is his," the empress said thoughtfully. "And what do you make of him? Do you know him well?"

Abbey hesitated. "Well, I know him, of course. He's not like anyone else."

"Does he wear armor? Is he large and powerful?" Prince Lothar demanded, leaning forward.

"Oh, no. Not at all. He wears a simple gray cloak. He's not as tall as you are, Prince."

"Then how does he command such loyalty?" the empress asked. "All over Nuworld he has followers. I cannot understand it. I've never met him. Can you explain it?"

"I think it must be that he has such love for his people."

The empress exchanged a quick glance with Prince Lothar. "That is it? He *loves* people? You mean the lords and ladies of nobility?"

"I don't think there are any 'nobles' in his kingdom, and he doesn't show any difference. Why, he shows just as much love to the lowest as he does to the most powerful warrior."

Lothar shifted uncomfortably. He wore a frown on his handsome face. "I cannot see how that would work," he said finally. "You must have discipline, and the only way to have that is to instill fear."

Abbey shook her head. "I don't think that is exactly right, Prince Lothar. The followers of Goél would do anything for him, but none of us are afraid of him—oh, maybe as a child is afraid of a father. But there is love there too."

The conversation went on for a long time. Abigail finally grew weary, and the empress, appearing to see this, said, "Well, we will have time to talk later. We are agreed that the truth is what we must have, are we not, Abigail?"

"Oh, yes. We must have the truth, always."

A smile touched the empress's lips. "We will talk more of this."

Abbey finished her meal, and then was fascinated by the entertainment. Acrobats turned fantastic flips, magicians made things disappear and reappear, so that she could not believe her eyes. There were dancers and singers, and she was utterly enraptured with the scene.

At length Abbey was introduced to the leading members of the Council—tall, stately men, some with hard eyes but all strong and wearing the sign of the serpent on their chests.

After the empress introduced Abbey, she said to the men, "She will be of great help to us in our struggle against the enemy." Then she looked at Lothar and whispered so softly that Abbey barely heard. "And a prince needs a princess, does he not?"

Lothar glanced over at Abbey and smiled. "Yes, My Empress," he said.

After the music and dancing, the empress said, "Now let me show you more of the palace."

It was a royal tour with just the empress and Abbey going through the passages. She saw marvelous things during the trip and said, "I could never find my way around, Your Majesty."

"Yes, it is a large palace. It took the labor of thousands and thousands to carve it out of solid stone. Others are busy finding the precious gems, but you have not seen the half."

Then Fareena said, "You must be tired. Let me take you to your quarters."

"Thank you, Your Majesty. I could never find my way alone."

When they were inside Abbey's room, the empress sat down for a moment. "I enjoy banquets," she said. "But a little quiet talk is sometimes much better, is it not?"

"Oh, yes, Your Majesty." Abbey still felt somewhat nervous in the presence of this beautiful woman. Her green eyes were so strong and powerful that she could not meet them, and she dropped her own gaze.

"Now I have a little gift for you." The empress reached into a hidden pocket and brought forth a small golden box. "My own special incense. I make it myself," she said proudly. Rising, she walked over to a table where an incense burner sat. She lit it from one of the candles, opened the golden box, and poured some of the incense into the bowl. "Come—we will enjoy it together," she said.

Abbey came to sit beside her, and soon the smoke from the incense rose from the burner.

"That is pleasant, is it not?"

"Oh, yes, very nice." Abbey actually thought the scent was rather strong, but she did not want to displease the empress. She continued to breathe the scented air, and for some reason it made her very sleepy.

She confessed this to the empress. "What is in it? It seems to make me drowsy."

"It's my own special formula," she said. "Better than any sleeping potion you will ever have. But it makes you feel very good, does it not?"

Abbey was sleepy. She had difficulty keeping her eyes open, and the empress's voice seemed to come from far away. But it was a rather delicious feeling.

"Have you noticed my pendant?" Empress Fareena asked softly, her voice no louder than a spring breeze. "It's beautiful, is it not?" The empress held it before her eyes.

Abigail stared at the green stone with the carving. "Yes," Abbey murmured. "Very beautiful."

"It was made for me many years ago by an expert craftsman. It's the only one of its kind. Do you see the carving?"

As the empress slowly let the pendant sway, Abbey tried to follow it. The deep green seemed to be magnified and the carved serpent almost alive.

"Very—very beautiful, Your Majesty," she muttered. It was growing harder and harder for her to stay awake.

The empress was speaking, and she tried desperately to keep her mind on what was being said. But that was more and more difficult. She did hear the empress say, "You have come to us to learn the truth, Abbey. You want the truth, do you not?"

"Yes—" Abbey nodded "—the truth."

The empress continued to speak about the Kingdom of the Underworld and its enemies the Underlings and how difficult it was to win the battle against them.

"But we must win, mustn't we, Abbey?"

"Yes, we must win."

"We can't let the evil ones take over the kingdom, can we?"

"No, we must not."

Again and again the empress spoke of truth and of the right way. Then she began to speak of what was to come. "If we can only defeat our enemies, you would receive great honor."

"Great honor?" Abigail echoed.

"Yes, more than you ever thought. These little trinkets that you wear—why, they're nothing. You love diamonds and jewels, do you not, Abbey?"

"Yes, I love them."

"They will all be yours, if you come to the truth."

"To the truth," Abigail recited obediently. On and on, the voice of the empress seemed to seep into her, and the green stone seemed to grow till it filled the room.

"I will make you strong, Abbey—and even more beautiful than you are now. You must trust me. You do trust me, don't you?"

"Yes, Your Majesty."

The scent of the incense, the flashing of the green stone, and the rhythmic voice of the Empress of the Underworld continued until Abbey's mind seemed to float and she was aware of only the empress.

How long this went on, she later had no idea. She woke to find herself in the bed with no memory of having undressed. She was wearing a beautiful nightgown, and the covers were pulled over her.

She raised her head, slightly sick from the odor of the incense, and called out, "Luna, are you there?"

Instantly the door to the chamber opened, lights came on, and the old woman whispered, "Yes, my lady, is there something you want?"

"Where is the empress?"

"She is gone. Shall I call her for you?"

"No, I feel a little sick, Luna. May I have a glass of water?"

"Yes, my lady." Luna returned soon with a glass of cool, sparkling water. She helped Abbey sit up and gave her the drink.

As Abbey lay back she said, "I don't remember the empress leaving. I don't remember much of anything except the green necklace she wore and the incense."

"Shall I sit by you for a while?"

"Please. I'm a little—a little lonesome."

Luna sat down and said quietly, "You are a long way from your home and friends. It's natural for you to be lonesome."

"Tell me about the empress."

"What do you want to hear, my lady?"

"She's very strange." Something about the last audience with the empress disturbed Abbey. "I don't—I don't know what to think about her. She kept talking about the truth."

Luna hesitated and said, "Yes, she talks a lot about the truth, the empress does."

"What does she mean by truth, Luna?"

"That is hardly for me to say."

Something in her tone caught at Abbey, and she turned her head and saw the lined face of the old woman. "Does it have something to do with the Underlings?"

Luna smiled slightly. "Yes, it does."

"Please tell me."

Luna hesitated again. "We are not allowed to speak of such things. If I were to tell you, and the empress found out, I would be sent to the mines. To the lower mines."

"What is there?"

"Some of the stones that you wore tonight were dug from deep, deep underground. People who are sent there are never released. They're chained to stakes and dig their lives out in darkness like moles."

"How awful! But what does that have to do with Empress Fareena?"

"I cannot tell." For one moment, the eyes of Luna gleamed, and then she said, "There are many who go around proclaiming that they have the truth, but many of these are false."

Abbey was growing sleepy again. "Then how am I to know what is the truth?"

"You must be very careful, Lady Abbey. Not all that glitters is gold."

"I've heard that before," Abbey said sleepily. "One of my friends told me that I like to look on the outside of things too much and not enough on the inside."

"That was a wise friend," Luna said quickly. "I would hold onto that if I were you."

"But what is the truth? Can't you just tell me?"

"Truth is hard to find. You know Goél?"

"Yes, of course."

"Then keep what he has told you in your heart. Others will tell you that they have the truth, but believe them not if it violates what you have been taught by him."

Then Abbey could stay awake no longer. Luna was a shapeless form as she began to drift off into sleep. She fell back into the soft bed, and her mind closed as if the sun had gone down. It was a warm darkness, but during the night she had dreams once again, mostly of a green stone with a snake carved in it and of the Empress of the Underworld.

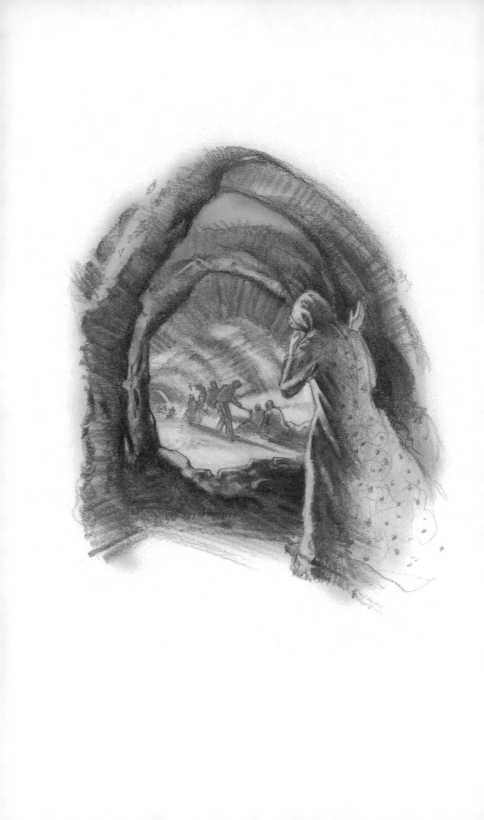

6
Abbey Sees the "Truth"

One day faded into another for Abbey. She had never seen such fabulous things as Lothar showed her. Almost every day there was an excursion, once to a sapphire mine, the next day a thrilling trip to an underground river, and—more than once—visits to the homes of the lords of the Underworld, all very thrilling to Abbey.

Every evening the empress would send for her or would sometimes even stop by her quarters. This surprised Abbey, for she had assumed that empresses did not make private calls.

But the empress seemed to be fond of her. Daily she would bring a new gift. A pair of exquisite shoes made of some sort of leather, softer than any she had ever seen. A bracelet of purple stones that seemed to glow with fire deep inside.

"These came from the deep mines, my dear. Some of our finest stones come from there."

"The deep mines?" Abbey recalled hearing of these. "Could we go there, Your Majesty? I'd love to see stones like this being dug out."

"Oh, it wouldn't be at all entertaining or amusing for you." The empress laughed. "Down there it is very dirty and hot. There are much more interesting things to see on the upper levels."

Abbey often wondered about the other Sleepers.

One night when the empress came, Abbey said, "I'm worried about my friends. I left them a note, but their journey may have taken longer than I'd thought. Do you suppose I could write them another letter?"

"Of course you could, Abbey." Empress Fareena smiled. She had very red lips, and her greenish eyes rolled as she nodded. "You have paper and pen. We'll send them by special courier."

"Oh, thank you, Your Majesty. That would be very kind. I'm—I'm a little lonely."

"Only natural, I'm sure. After all, you seven have been very close, haven't you?"

"Oh, yes. We're a family really."

"Tell me some more of your exciting tales," Empress Fareena said. She sat down in a chair across from Abbey and listened as the girl told her more of the adventures of the Sleepers.

Even as she was speaking, however, Abbey touched her temples. "I don't know, Your Majesty. It all seems a little vague now. I—I seem to be losing my memory."

The empress reached over, as she did every night, and lit the incense burner. At once the air began to carry its sharp, aromatic fragrance.

Now she turned to Abbey, and her voice grew soft. "Perhaps it's because you are learning more about the way things really are." She took up the gold chain that held the green jewel and began to let it swing slowly. She waited till the girl's eyes were fixed upon it, then said, "We have been happy to have you with us, but time grows short, doesn't it?"

Abbey nodded, her eyes fastened on the stone. "Yes, Your Majesty." She sounded as if she were in a deep sleep—which indeed she was.

For a long time the empress spoke of many things.

Something like this had happened for several nights, and each time she had awakened to find herself in bed.

Tonight she heard the empress's voice coming from far away. "My dear Abbey, you will be a princess, for you are coming to know the truth. You do know the truth, Abbey."

"Yes, I know the truth."

She awakened sometime later. As usual, she was in bed. Her head hurt, and her thoughts swirled. Tossing the covers back, she stepped out onto the floor and began to walk back and forth.

"If there were only a window I could look out of, I might see the stars or a tree," she whispered, knowing she would not. She stopped abruptly, for this was a longing that she had not expressed before. For all the beauty of the jewels and the richness of her surroundings, still she missed the green grass, the blue skies, and the touch of soft wind on her cheek.

Suddenly Abbey became upset. Quickly she dressed in her riding outfit. She longed to be alone, and there was one place she had found to be quite solitary.

Abbey saw as she passed through her outer chamber that Luna was asleep, and she did not awaken her. Outside, she looked to see if there were any guards, but there were none—or they were making their rounds in another part of the palace.

She made her way quickly down silent halls that glowed with the same eerie green glint that she had come to dislike. After making several turns, she came to a door, and when she opened it she found herself outside the palace proper. Here there were no jewels, no diamonds, and the light was not so bright. She walked for a time along the walls, and her feeling of loneliness became stronger.

"I'd give anything if I could see Josh. Or Sarah. Or see Reb throw his rope over an animal's head. And how I miss Wash and Dave. I wish they'd come. I wish—"

A figure suddenly stepped from an entranceway, and Abbey cried out in fear.

The figure halted, and a gravelly voice said, "It's only me, ma'am."

The figure came closer, and Abbey saw that the man was carrying a large bag on his back. At first she had thought he was hunchbacked. She breathed with relief and said, "You frightened me!"

"I didn't mean to do that, ma'am. Just old Bono on my way down."

"You're going down?"

"Down to the deep mines, I am." He was an older man with white hair and a wrinkled face, but he had a pair of blue eyes that were alert. He wore rags and was dirty from head to foot. "Didn't mean to disturb you, ma'am," he said and moved to go on.

"Wait! I'd like to go with you."

"Oh, that wouldn't be possible!" The old man seemed to be shocked. "None of the nobility ever go to the deep mines."

"I'd like to see them," Abbey insisted.

Bono shook his head. He pulled off his ragged cap and vigorously scratched his thatch of dusty white hair. "Well, ma'am, I can't say no. We slaves have to do what we're told. But you might get me in trouble."

"I won't tell. Just let me go."

Bono shrugged and said, "Well, I'm going, if you want to follow. I'd appreciate it if you didn't tell anyone how you found your way there."

"I won't tell."

Thus Abbey began a strange journey.

Bono trudged ahead, stooped over, bearing his heavy bag. She could hear his wheezing as they moved steadily downhill.

The incline grew steeper and steeper, until finally it was difficult to keep her balance. They passed by several levels that led off from the descending stairway, but Bono did not say a word. Was the air growing thinner? It grew harder for her to breathe, and she wanted to turn back. It was darker too. Now only flickering lanterns hanging from steel pegs gave any light at all.

Finally Bono turned to her and said, "Better not go any deeper, ma'am."

"Is this the deep mine?"

"It's the first of it, ma'am. It'd hardly be safe to go farther. It's hard to breathe here, ain't it now?"

"Yes, it is."

"I'll be going, but you'd best stay here. It wouldn't be safe."

Bono left and, for one moment, Abbey was ready to turn and climb back up to the palace. Still, curiosity overcame her, and she approached the doorway that was chiseled into the solid rock. She moved cautiously, for here the floor was treacherous with loose stones and dirt. This was no elaborately carved passage but literally a rough tunnel like one dug by a huge mole.

Ahead she saw a light and heard voices. Carefully and silently she crept ahead. When she got close enough, she was shocked to see two women digging with pickaxes, while two children loaded rocks into a small wagon.

By the wavering light she could see that the women were past middle age. Their hands were splayed as they held the axes, and it appeared to take all their strength to break off even a tiny fragment of rock. The children were pale-faced and listless. They looked starved, like their mothers.

Why, they look like refugees from old Nazi prisons that I've seen in history books, Abbey thought with shock. As she listened, the workers said little. When they did speak, there was no hope in their voices at all.

"My-Ling died this morning," one woman said. She spoke slowly, as if every word was a burden.

The other woman waited for a time. She lifted her pick, struck the tunnel wall, and loosed a fragment no bigger than a marble. Then she leaned against the wall, breathing hard. "She's better off, poor soul. I wish I was with her."

One of the children, a little girl, reached up and took her mother's ragged garment in her hand. "We'll be with her soon, won't we, Mother?"

The worn woman turned her face to the child, and Abbey had never seen such a hopeless expression in her whole life. The woman's eyes and cheeks were sunken. When she spoke, her voice was a mere whisper. "Yes, soon. And that will be good."

Abbey made her way quietly back up to the entrance to the deep mines. She felt stricken. Never had she seen such hopelessness, and something close to hatred rose in her to think that women and children would be treated like this.

"Worse than animals," she fumed as she moved up the passage. She saw no one on the way, and by the time she got back to her room she was very disturbed. Entering, she was suddenly shocked, for there stood the empress!

Empress Fareena smiled. "I've been waiting for you. Been out for a little walk?"

"Y-Yes, Your Majesty."

"A little late for an excursion, isn't it, my dear?"

"I couldn't sleep."

The empress's eyes glittered. "Come. Sit down. We must talk."

Against her will, Abbey sat.

The empress sat across from her, as was her custom. "Something troubling you, my dear?"

"Yes, Your Majesty. I suppose I shouldn't have done it, but I wandered down into the lower parts."

"To the deep mines?"

"Not all the way, Your Majesty. But deep enough. Oh, what I saw was awful!"

"Oh, my dear, I suppose you saw some of the slaves. It is sad, isn't it?"

"Why do women and children have to be chained and made to work in that awful place?"

"No one hates the thought of that worse than I, my dear. But you must understand that the forces against us are powerful. We must not give in one inch."

"But children? How could they—"

"I know how it looks." The empress held up a hand and shook her head sadly. "Let me explain to you."

The empress began speaking about how difficult it was to be an empress. And how evil was coming into the Kingdom of the Underworld and how cruel things must sometimes be done.

"We must be cruel to be kind," she said. "One day the Underlings will see truth, and then, of course, we will bring them out into freedom. But right now they do not see the truth." The voice grew softer, and Abbey once again found herself looking at the writhing snake on the green stone, which the empress moved back and forth.

The woman spoke softly until Abbey almost felt herself being—*invaded.* Abbey was a very private person. She valued her freedom and independence, and this frightened her. She tried to cry out, but she could not.

"Now it is time for you to know the truth. You have served Goél, have you not?"

"Yes, yes."

"And I know you did it with a good heart, but the truth we have tried to bring to you and must now give you is that Goél is not what you think. He is the enemy of freedom, the enemy of peace. It is he that keeps the slaves in chains in the deep mines. All the troubles in Nuworld come from Goél."

"No, no, that can't be!" Abbey gasped.

The incense grew stronger, and the sense of being controlled grew more powerful.

"Ah, you have been deceived. But you must not fear. You love your friends—these other Sleepers?"

"Oh, yes!"

"Then you must save them from Goél as we have saved you and given you the truth. You must do the same for them."

Abbey never remembered clearly what happened. Over and over again she heard the words "You must save your friends. You must tell them the truth. Goél is leading them into disaster. Only I can help, the Empress of the Underworld." Finally Abbey felt totally helpless. "How can I help them?" she whispered.

"Ah, I'm glad to hear you have such feelings. You must write them a message. 'Come and save me, for I'm in danger.' And you must ask them to come at once."

"'Come at once,'" Abbey repeated.

"Here is paper and a pen. Write them and beg them to come and save you."

The incense grew even more dense. Abbey's mind seemed to be paralyzed. All she could hear was the voice of the Empress of the Underworld, and she wrote the letter slowly, begging the other Sleepers to come and save her.

"There. Now lie down and sleep. You have found the truth." She helped the girl to the bed, smiled down at her, and whispered, "We have you now, Miss Abigail."

The empress picked up the message. Then she turned and left the room.

Fareena went at once down the hall to where Lothar was waiting for her.

"The Dark Lord—he is here," he said in a voice not steady.

The empress smiled. "Do not be afraid. The girl has given in. Come."

The two proceeded down another hall. The empress pressed a button. A secret door opened, and they found themselves in a large room where a cloaked figure stood in the semidarkness. Only the light from a single candle illuminated the room faintly.

"Have you accomplished the task I gave you?" The voice was harsh and rang with power.

Empress Fareena blinked, but she smiled. "Yes, O Master of Darkness. The girl has sent for her friends. They will come, and once they pass through the doors of the Underworld, we will have them."

Lothar nodded. "Yes, Sire, no one escapes from our kingdom."

The Dark Lord's eyes were reddish under the cowl that he wore. "See that you do not fail." His lips turned up in a cruel smile. "If you do, we will have to take stern measures, even with you, Empress Fareena, and you, Prince Lothar."

His threat hung in the air, and as the two bowed out, both of them—stout as they were—knew fear at the very center of their bones.

7

Josh's Dream

The party that filed out of the heavy forest was ragged and worn. Looking back, Zohar paused and said to Josh, walking behind him, "Was hard mission." He grunted. "We lose three good men."

There were circles under Josh's eyes, and he'd lost weight. The mission had been terribly difficult. All of them were drained. And now as he looked at the thatch-roofed house, he expelled a deep breath. "I'm glad to be here again."

Tam and Mat, the Gemini twins, were right behind him. "Now we'll get something to eat," Tam said cheerfully. He poked a hole through his leather jerkin, adding, "And I can do a little patchwork so I can be handsome again."

"You never were handsome." Mat scowled. "And we're not going to get anything good to eat. It's been the worst mission I was ever on!"

Dave came up. He too was worn down, and he looked at Mat with disgust. "You say that after every mission."

Josh said, "We'll get cleaned up and have a meal, and then we'll feel better." He slapped each friend on the back and encouraged them all. "You did fine, Reb. Couldn't have done it without you. Wash, you all right? Sure you are!"

He gave Sarah a close look and shook his head. "I know you're tired, but we can rest awhile now." He fell in step beside her and noted that her legs seemed to be trembling. He wanted to help her but knew she would re-sent any offer. "It's been hard on all of us," he said, then added, "You did fine, Sarah."

"So did you, Josh." Sarah's face was drawn with fatigue, but she found a smile. She poked her finger through a rent in his shirt and said, "I'll have to get my needle and thread out again."

They entered the compound, and the families came running out to meet the warriors. For a while there was excitement, and then the women began preparing a meal.

Dave was looking around. "I don't see Abbey," he said. "I thought she'd be out to meet us."

"So did I." Josh frowned. "Sarah, do you feel like climbing up and seeing if she's still asleep?"

"In the middle of the morning?" Sarah shook her head. "I doubt it."

At that moment, Zohar came stalking toward them. He had a piece of paper in his hand and thrust it at Josh. "For you," he grunted, then walked off.

"This is Abbey's writing," Josh said. He opened the paper and read the message aloud.

I wish you were here; but since you were gone, I had to make a decision. I have gone to the Kingdom of the Underworld with Prince Lothar. They are in need of our help. As soon as I get there, I will send word with a map so you can follow.

"Well, I like that!" Wash snapped. "She goes waltzing off on a mission all by herself when she wouldn't go with us!"

"I'd like to see that prince," Sarah said grimly. "I bet he's a lulu."

"What do you mean by that?" Reb asked in surprise.

"I mean, I bet everything I've got against a hat pin that he's a good-looking dude. I can't think of any other reason why she'd go."

"Oh, don't be too hard on her, Sarah," Dave said. He reached out his hand and took the letter, then scratched his head. "It is a little bit mysterious, though. Let's go find out more about this Prince Lothar and this place called the Underworld. Doesn't sound healthy to me."

They made their way to where Zohar sat before the fire watching some meat roasting. Josh read him the letter, then asked, "Do you know anybody named Lothar?"

"No, but the Underworld not a good place."

The Sleepers exchanged troubled glances. "You know about it, Zohar?"

"Yes."

"Well, what's the matter with it?" Sarah demanded.

"Yes, and where is it?" Wash asked. "Is it really underground?"

Zohar gave them a strange look. "I never there, but we lose people. The empress, she make slaves of everyone she gets."

"Slaves?" Josh asked sharply. "What happens to them?"

Zohar shrugged his massive shoulders. "They go underground. Never know anybody to come up."

"Well, that doesn't sound good," Dave said ruefully. He looked at Zohar. "What about this Lothar? Does anyone know what he looks like?"

Zohar questioned all his people but found out nothing.

"So we don't know what he looks like or where they've gone, and we don't know why she went," Jake said. He looked around impatiently. "We should have just tied her and made her go with us!"

"Too late to talk about what we should've done," Josh said wearily. "What we've got to talk about is what we *can* do."

"We'll have to go after her," Sarah said.

Josh looked at Zohar. "Can you take us there?"

Zohar shook his head. "We wait for Goél's word. Place is hidden underground. Nobody knows how to get there."

This bit of information dismayed Josh. He ran his hand through his auburn hair and looked despondent. "I wish Goél would come. I don't know what to do."

Dave was very practical. "There's really nothing to do but wait, Josh. We can't go tearing off into the jungle, not knowing where we're going."

"Dave's right," Sarah said. "We'll just have to wait." She looked down at her tattered clothes. "One thing we can do is get rested and get into better outfits."

"That's right," Reb said. "I don't want to be tackling a whole kingdom without something to fight with."

In the end, the Sleepers forced themselves to rest a great deal. The hunting had been good, so the food strengthened them. A week went by and then another. Still no word from Abbey—or from Goél.

Josh almost worried himself sick.

Sarah said, "You've got to learn to wait, Josh. I know it's hard. But soon the time for action will come, and you've got to be fresh."

Josh forced himself to grin. "Why is it that you're always right and I'm always wrong?"

"That's not true. I've been wrong lots of times, and you're nearly always right, Josh. It's just that you're feeling this responsibility. You've had it ever since we came to this place. It'd be hard on anybody."

Josh shrugged his shoulders. "You're right, of course. We'll just have to wait. I'll stuff myself and sleep, and sooner or later we'll get a message. Then we can go."

That very night Josh lay on his cot, tossing and turning. It was warm, and he found great difficulty in going to sleep. He looked across the room where the moonlight was filtering through the window. It illuminated the still forms of the other boys, all of them dead to the world.

Why can't I go to sleep like that? Josh thought. *It's miserable staying awake like this. I'll try counting sheep.* He counted up to two thousand sheep, then thought, *That's no good. I'll try counting dinosaurs. T-Rexes, maybe.* This was no better. It only brought back memories of when he'd barely escaped with his life from the teeth of such monsters in the land of the cavemen.

Finally he did drift off, but it was not into a sound sleep. Images flitted through his mind, some of which he could not identify. Many of them were from past adventures he'd had with the other Sleepers. Once he saw the Snakepeople—beings that had upright bodies but heads like serpents, their fangs glistening with poison. He wakened, rolled over, and forced that image from his mind. Sleep would not come again for a long time.

Then he fell into one of those modes where he knew he was dreaming and could not separate himself from the dream. He tried to wake up but could not. Sweat popped out on his forehead, and he writhed and tossed on his bunk.

In the dream he was in a cave of total blackness. He was crawling along on his hands and knees. The dream seemed so real that he could feel the sharp stones bite into the palms of his hands and cut into his knees. He had never liked dark, closed spaces, and such fear came over him that he wanted to call out.

Faster and faster he scrambled, trying to find his way out. There were many turns and twists. And each time he thought he was almost out and would soon see a light, always there was only darkness. It was like being buried alive. He struggled on forever, it seemed.

Then finally, far up ahead, he saw movement and a

faint flickering. With a glad cry, he scuttled forward. The tunnel enlarged, and he yelled, "Hello, anybody there?"

But when he came to the light, he saw a sight that froze his blood. He saw figures all chained together by their ankles, swinging axes at the solid rock. Their faces were dull and their eyes lifeless. They looked like the zombies he had seen in movies back in Oldworld. The sight frightened him so badly that he cried aloud and ran down a side passage. He seemed to be running to the center of the earth.

Then he saw another light. He started running toward it as fast as he could. This time the light was brighter, and he now could see two figures, one clothed in white and one clothed in black.

"Help! Help me!" he shouted. He stumbled forward, then was shocked to realize that the figure in white was Abbey.

"Abbey! Help me!" he cried. "I'm lost!"

But Abbey did not even look at him. It was as if she had not heard. She was dressed in a fine white dress, and she wore jewels on her fingers and in her hair. There was something frightening about the emptiness in her face.

"She looks like those slaves. What's *wrong* with her?" Josh asked in agony. "Abbey!" he cried out. "Wake up!"

And then the figure dressed in black turned to him. It was a woman. She had green eyes that glittered as they fixed themselves on him. She reached down slowly with her long white fingers and clutched the large green stone that hung at her breast.

"You must know the truth," she said and smiled. There was something terrible in her smile.

Josh stopped abruptly. Somehow in his dream he felt the power of the green stone reach out to him like the empress's long finger. It touched him, and he felt himself grow cold. Then he felt the power of the strange woman grasp him with an icy fist.

And he knew why Abbey looked so blank, her eyes so dead. She was in the power of this mysterious evil woman.

With a wild cry, Josh threw himself backward and ran into the darkness of the tunnel, and the voice of the woman in black came after him. "We will have you. We will have all of the Sleepers."

Josh had never been so frightened in his life. He yelled and suddenly opened his eyes.

Dave and Reb and Jake and Wash were standing over him.

"What's the matter, Josh? You having a nightmare?" Reb asked anxiously.

They were all holding him down, and Josh realized he was trembling. He took a deep breath and nodded. "It's OK. You can let me up now."

When he sat up on the bed, Wash said, "Boy, that must have been the granddaddy of nightmares! I never heard anybody scream like you did."

"What was it?" Jake demanded. "You eat something that didn't agree with you?"

But Dave was looking into Josh's face. "What is it, Josh? It's more than just a bad dream, isn't it?"

Josh drew his hand across his face. "I think it is. I think it tells us something about what has happened to Abbey. Listen, and I'll tell you about the dream."

The four stood around him as Josh described his dream. He could see it as clearly as if it were before him. When he ended, his voice was not steady.

"Abbey looked dead. Her eyes had no life in them. And whoever that woman was, she was out to get me too." He hesitated, then reached over and pulled a cloth from the pocket of his pants lying on the floor. He wiped

71

his face with it. "I think I met the Empress of the Underworld, and I think Abbey's in worse trouble than any of us thought."

Dave stared at Josh, then looked around the circle. When he spoke, it was to say, "Well, that complicates things, doesn't it?"

"What do you mean, Dave?" Reb inquired.

"I mean, we heard from Zohar that once someone goes to that place called the Underworld, they never come back. So when we hear from Abbey, what do we do? Go after her?"

Josh stared at him. "We'll have to."

Dave Cooper had his share of courage, but he, like Josh and Sarah, had a fear of being in close places. He shook his head and said, "That would be a hard thing, Josh. I would rather go almost anywhere than down a hole in the ground like that."

Josh nodded. "Me too, Dave. But she's one of the Seven. We'll have to go when she sends for us."

A heaviness fell over the group, as all realized that sooner or later they would have to go into the Kingdom of the Underworld.

8
Reb Sets a Trap

I wish you'd watch what you're doing, Wash," Reb snapped irritably. "You left your stuff all over my bunk."

Wash looked up from where he was sitting on his own cot, reading a small book. He was the mildest mannered of all the Sleepers, but now he glared at Reb. "You're a fine one to talk. You scatter your stuff around like a junkman!"

For a minute, Reb seemed ready to get up and go to war, then he chuckled. "If we have to wait much longer, we're going to start the Civil War all over again." He walked over to the window and stared out. "I sure do hate this waiting," he complained gloomily. "Sometimes I think we ought to just start out looking for that place—that Underworld."

Wash had calmed down by now too. He put his book down and came over to stare out the window with Reb. Outside, the trees were swaying from a stiff breeze.

Looking at the thick forest, the smaller boy shook his head. "That wouldn't do any good. We could wander forever looking for the entrance to that underground city. It'd be like looking for a needle in a haystack."

"I reckon so," Reb admitted. "But I think Josh is about to lose his mind. He's worse than any of us."

"That's because he's the leader," Wash said. "He feels responsible."

"Wasn't his fault Abigail wouldn't go with us."

"No, it's not. But he thinks it is—and sometimes that's just as bad."

Then Jake entered. "Got something to tell you," he said.

"What is it, Jake?" Reb asked. "Did we get word from Abbey?"

"No, not that. But something's going on around here."

"Going on? Like what?" Wash demanded.

Jake got the look on his face that both boys had learned to dislike. Jake was very smart, but he was also very difficult at times. When he knew something that none of the others did, he liked to stretch it out and let them wallow in their own ignorance, as he put it.

"If you wouldn't sleep so much," the redheaded youngster said, "maybe you'd know as much as I do."

"I don't sleep any more than you do," Wash argued. "What are you talking about?"

Reb frowned. "Aw, he don't know anything, Wash. He just likes to show off."

Jake straightened up. He was rather short anyway, and he resented Reb's tall stature. "That's all you know," he taunted. "If you knew what I know, you'd be a lot smarter. And if you'd listen to me more, you'd know more."

Reb slumped on his cot in disgust. "We know you can name all the capitals of the states, but that don't mean much—seeing that there ain't no states anymore. What is it this time?"

Jake teased them for a while but finally got serious. "I've been waking up at night for the last two nights. And you know that's not like me—I usually sleep pretty good."

The other two grinned at each other, then Reb nodded. "That's the truth! You sleep like you're dead. Never knew anything to wake you up."

"That's what bothers me." Jake scratched his head and went over to the window. He looked out. "Last night and the night before last, in the middle of the night, I thought I heard something. Well, I tried to go back to sleep, but I couldn't. So finally I got up and came over here to the window." He turned around, and now his face was serious. "Somebody was out there sneaking around."

"Probably one of Zohar's people. A guard, maybe."

"No, it wasn't anyone like that."

"How do you know?" Wash asked. "It was dark, and you couldn't see."

"If you'd stay up once in a while at night, you'd know that there was a full moon and the stars were out. It was real bright. I could see good."

Seeing the seriousness in Jake's face, Reb demanded, "Well, what did you see? Tell us about it."

"It was kind of strange," Jake admitted. "At first it was just kind of a shadow. Over there—right by that little grove of trees. I thought maybe it was a wild animal or a dog or something. But then I saw it was a man. He moved as if he was trying to hide. You know how it is when somebody does that. They don't just walk upright; they crouch over. Well, I watched him, and he moved around, and then he came over to the house. He came up under this window—and I guess he saw me. He took out running. He was a skinny sort of fellow. I couldn't see his face, but he made for the woods."

Wash was interested in the story. "I wonder who it could be."

"I don't know, but he was there early this morning again, right before dawn. I was more careful this time." Jake looked thoughtful. "He seems to be looking for something. He goes around looking in the windows. I was hoping he'd come to this one again, but he didn't. He's fast too. I don't think any of us could catch him, unless you had a horse, Reb."

When Dave and Josh came in, Jake repeated his story.

Josh said glumly, "Probably just one of the villagers.

Maybe some kid out looking for some mischief. Forget it, Jake. We've got more important things to do."

Josh left almost at once, and as soon as he was gone, Reb said, "I think Josh has missed too much sleep. He looks tired, and he's right snappy." He listened while the other boys talked, and finally he sat up straight on his bunk. "Hey, I've got an idea!" he exclaimed.

Jake grinned. "Just lie down, and it'll go away, Reb. Probably the first one you've ever had."

"Just listen, Jake. Just listen. I'll tell you what we're going to do . . ."

"You know, I think this might work," Wash said. He and Reb were outside in the semidarkness. Night was about ready to fall. The two of them had been out for about an hour looking for a place to try Reb's scheme.

"Sure, it'll work." Reb nodded confidently. He was looking at a slender sapling that rose high in the air. It stood alone in a clearing, having been left there for some reason or another when other trees were chopped down for firewood and to make huts.

Reb looked up at the tall, swaying tree. "Now you climb up the tree and go all the way to the top."

Wash looked up. "I don't know. That's pretty tall. I could fall and break my pretty neck."

Reb grinned and said, "If you do, I'll go get Dave to do it. Go on, now. You can climb a little old tree."

Wash looked dubious. However, he began to climb, almost in slow motion.

"Hurry up, Wash," Reb called impatiently, looking up at the boy. "We haven't got all night. Get with it!"

Wash glared at his friend but began to climb faster. As he ascended the tree, it began to sway back and forth. The swaying made him a little giddy, but he managed to hold on.

"All the way to the top," Reb called. "Make it bend over."

"I'm going as fast as I can—but this thing's making me seasick!"

"You mean treesick, don't you?" Reb laughed at his own joke, but Wash wasn't amused. He was almost to the top when suddenly his weight caused the tree to droop over.

"Hang on," Reb said. "I'll get you!"

The treetop bowed down with the small boy clinging to it. Wash suddenly felt a rope settle around his legs and draw tight. He knew that Reb had lassoed him. Then he felt Reb pulling on the rope, and he yelled, "Be careful! Don't pull me off this thing!"

"I've got you now," Reb said. He pulled Wash and the treetop down. Wash freed his legs, and Reb snubbed the tree with his rope. "Now help me hold it."

The two boys gripped the rope that held the tree down. With one hand Reb pounded a stake into the ground. Quickly he wrapped the rope around the stake, saying, "Now, we're going to set the noose right over here."

He dug a shallow trench and began putting the rest of the rope in it. "Cover it up with dirt," he said.

When they got to the end of the rope, he made a slip knot and carefully arranged the loop in a circular ditch about two feet in diameter. Then he covered that with dirt, stepped back, and said, "Now, we make the trigger." He rigged a trigger that was both efficient and clever.

"How do you know how to do this?" Wash asked curiously.

"Why, shoot! I've caught about a million rabbits like this in my time. The rabbit steps in that loop, hits the trigger and—*bang!*—the tree pops up and jerks the noose tight. Usually catches the rabbit right around the neck. But I reckon this one we'll catch around the leg."

"Is that all there is to it?"

"All except one thing. It come to me that fellow might be looking for food, so we're going to leave a little bait out here."

"What kind of bait?"

"I'll show you." The taller boy led the way to the knapsack where he kept his equipment, pulled out a jug, and held it up. "Here's the bait."

"Whatcha got in there?"

"Nothing but some goat milk. But if that fellow's hungry and looking for something to eat, he'll try anything. So my thinking is, he'll see this jug and come over and investigate. When he does, he'll step in this noose, touch the trigger, and—*zing*—there he is! Dangling up in the tree like an apple."

Wash looked around. "I hope it works, but we'd better get out of here. He won't come while we're standing over the bait."

The two boys checked the trap, then went into the house.

"We're going to have to take turns sitting up," Reb said. "I want to find out who that fellow is. He'll probably holler when the trap snatches him up, but if it catches him by the neck, we might hang him by mistake."

"I'll take the first watch," Wash said quickly. "You guys go to bed, and I'll wake somebody up."

Josh was staring moodily at the pair and shook his head. "You're just playing games. Nobody's going to be out there—or you might get an innocent person." He lay down on his bed, saying grumpily, "Leave me out of it."

Wash stayed up for two hours, growing very sleepy. Then he awakened Reb, who got up and took his place.

Wash went to sleep at once, but it seemed he had barely closed his eyes when Reb woke him by calling out, "Yippee! We got our rabbit!"

All of the boys were awakened by Reb's loud yelp, and they lurched to their feet, bleary-eyed with sleep.

Reb started for the door. "Come on. Let's see what we got."

Josh stumbled outside, noticing that the night was very bright. The moon was high in the sky, like a huge silver coin. Then he looked across the yard and saw something moving in the top of the tall sapling.

"We got him!" Wash yelled. "We got him!"

"We sure did." Reb grinned. He shook out a lariat, made a couple of easy turns around his head, then threw the rope upward. He was almost infallible with a rope. Whatever he threw it at, he caught.

In the moonlight Josh saw a figure struggling, caught by one foot and waving his arms around. The rope fell over his upper body, and Reb pulled it tight. "Quiet down, up there!" he said. "We'll take care of you."

The four boys easily pulled the sapling over again. When their captive was on the ground, Reb released the ropes and let the tree fly back upward.

Josh was holding onto the intruder, a tall, rather thin young man with large eyes. He was so dirty and ragged that it was hard to tell much else about him. "Who are you and what do you want, sneaking around here?" Josh demanded.

The captive stared at Josh, and for a moment Josh thought he'd say nothing. "My name is Beren," he gasped finally.

"What are you doing sneaking around here, Beren?" Reb asked. "You could've gotten hanged by that rope."

"You're not from around here, are you?" Dave demanded.

"I've never seen you before," Jake said. He stepped closer. "Are you a spy of the Dark Lord or something?"

At those words, the young man called Beren, who appeared to be fifteen or sixteen, shook his head. "No, I do not serve the Dark Lord."

"Well, who are you then? Where are you from?" Josh asked. Then he stopped. "I didn't mean to be so rough on you," he said. "But we're having some trouble here, and we're a little bit nervous. Here, let me take these ropes off."

He freed the young man, but Reb kept a tight grip on his arm.

"Hold him," Jake said. "He's faster than any guy you ever saw. I've seen him run."

"Turn him loose, Reb. He's not an enemy," Josh commanded. He waited till Reb obeyed, then said again, "Didn't mean to treat you so rough, Beren." He looked at the boy. "You look hungry. Come on in, and we'll scare up something to eat."

The young man did not argue. "I am hungry," he admitted.

Soon they were in the boys' room.

Beren hungrily ate the cold meat and bread that was set before him and washed it down with goat's milk. At last he looked down at the plate and said, "That's the first time I've eaten in a long time."

"Are you ready to tell us a little something now?" Josh asked in a kindly fashion. The boy was so ragged and scared-looking that he didn't seem to present any danger. "Are you a runaway?"

Beren laughed at him. "In a way I am." He held out his hands, and Josh saw the chafe marks on his wrists. "I was chained, but I managed to escape—something that's never happened before."

"Escape from where?" Jake prodded.

Beren looked at him and answered simply, "From the

Kingdom of the Underworld. I was a slave there—what they call an Underling."

"The *Underworld!*" Josh exclaimed. "That's where we need to go."

Beren straightened up, and his eyes grew brighter. "Are you part of the Sleepers? I know that there are seven of you, although one will not be here."

"How do you know that?" Josh demanded.

"Because the young woman is a prisoner of the Empress of the Underworld."

At once the boys all started throwing questions at Beren, who simply became confused.

Finally Josh held up a hand. "Quiet, everybody! He can't hear all of us at once." When they calmed down, he said, "Tell us about the girl. Her name is Abbey, and she is one of us. There's another young woman here in another room."

Beren began to speak rapidly. He told about his escape from the deep mines, where most of the slaves were kept.

"We have heard of the Seven Sleepers. Somehow the rumor came that you were here. We heard also that Lothar had come to lead you into a trap—to capture you. So I came as quick as I could, but the young woman would not believe me, and Lothar drove me away. Then he took her away on fast horses. I could do no more but wait for you," he said finally.

Josh had listened carefully to the story. "Tell us about the Underworld," he said. "More about Lothar and the empress."

"She is not the true empress. She has put a spell on the inhabitants. She and Lothar rule, but the true Royal Family is kept in a special prison." He drew himself up then, and there was something regal about his look. "I am the true prince. They wanted to kill me, but Lothar thought

I would be of some use as a hostage. So they put me to work in the deep mines. I almost died there."

He went on to describe the awful conditions of the mines and how the empress with her spells had clouded the minds of the Council and other leaders. "She's an evil sorceress," he said bitterly. "And her powers are great."

"Will you take us to the Kingdom of the Underworld?" Josh asked.

Beren smiled. "That is why I came—seeking your help." He looked around at the five young men. "We'll need an army. But even an army will have trouble overcoming the Underworld. There are traps, and they have powerful forces. We must find some other way than mere battle."

They talked until almost dawn.

At last Josh said, "We've left before on missions like this—when we didn't know the end of our journey or whether we'd ever come back."

Beren said, "I believe I am the only one who has ever escaped from the evil empress's Underworld. Others just die there. Once the door closes, you're in darkness forever."

"Goél will not fail us," Josh said. "I know he would have us go. We'll get our weapons and provisions, and we'll leave at once."

As the sun arose that morning, six of the Seven Sleepers, led by Beren—who had been clothed in better dress—left the village. They made their way along a jungle trail.

Josh knew that every one of them was thinking the same thing. *Will we be able to save Abbey? And how can we defeat the Empress of the Underworld?*

9
Worms!

"Are you sure this is the place, Beren?" Josh asked.

The small band had traveled hard since leaving the village, and all were weary. Now Josh looked about at the underbrush and the sheer face of the wall that stood before them. "I was looking for something a little more impressive than this."

Beren nodded firmly. "Right down that way about a half mile you'll find a gate. But we can't go in that way."

"Why not?" Dave asked.

"Because it's the front door of the kingdom, and it will be well guarded. Besides," Beren added, "it has a spell on it, and only the servants of the empress know how to break the spell and cause the door to open."

"I expect that fellow Lothar knew it all right," Josh said. He looked both ways, then down at the ground. "It's hard to believe that there's all you say underneath where we're standing. It looks just like any other kind of ground to me."

"The Kingdom of the Underworld is not obvious." Beren leaned against the wall of stone and took a deep breath. "We have been content in the past to live our own lives. Our contact with the surface dwellers has been limited."

Wash had been walking up and down while Beren gave them this information. Now he said, "Well, how do you get into the Underworld then, Beren?"

"I will show you." He moved along the base of the

rock and, coming to a pile of shale and small boulders, nodded. "It's right here."

As the Sleepers gathered around, Mat complained, "Looks like a pile of rocks to me. I don't think there's anything there."

"I do," Tam said cheerfully. "You want me to move some of that stone for you, Beren?"

"Yes. We keep this entrance carefully covered. Only two or three people in the Royal Family know about it."

Uncovering the entrance did not take long, for when the Gemini Twins and the boys did not make much headway, Volka grunted, "Ho, move aside." With his huge hands he began pulling at the rocks. *"Hroom!"* Soon he had laid bare a tiny entrance. "There."

Beren grinned. "I don't think it's big enough for you. You ought to make it bigger, Volka. But this is the place!"

When Volka had enlarged the hole, Beren said, "This is a dangerous way." His eyes grew serious. "Watch out for the worms."

Reb stared at him, then scoffed. "Worms! Why, I use them for fish bait. I'm not afraid of any old worm."

"These worms are different," Beren said grimly.

"How different?" Sarah asked tentatively. She shivered a little. "I never could stand to put a worm on a fish hook."

Beren hesitated, then said, "You wouldn't put these on a fish hook, Sarah. They're enormous—and dangerous."

"What do they look like?" Jake demanded.

"They look pretty bad," Beren said. "In the first place, they're big—about a foot or more in diameter. And sometimes up to twenty feet long."

Reb whistled. "Boy, that *would* be fish bait."

"And another thing—they're poisonous. They have an ugly-looking head with horns, and in those horns are poison sacs. They'll strike at you like a snake, and if they nail you with one of those horns and pump poison into you, well—there's not much that could be done."

Sarah stared at Beren, then shivered again. "Is there any *other* way in besides this one?"

"No. But the good part is that the guards of the empress don't come this way. They're afraid of the worms."

"Well," Josh said quickly, seeing the apprehension in the eyes of his friends, "we'll be all right. Get your swords out, and if we see any of them, we'll fight together."

"That's the best way," Beren agreed. He pulled something that looked like sticks out of his pack and passed them around. "These are special torches," he said. "They're soaked with oil, and the tips will burn for about an hour. It'll be very dark at first, but later on it will be better. Are you ready?"

"Let's go," Josh said. "We've seen bad things before, and Goél will help us."

Beren lit his torch, and the others ignited theirs. Beren then turned and slipped into the hole in the ground. The Sleepers followed with Volka bringing up the rear. He had a difficult time wriggling through the small hole and had to enlarge it even more. The others waited.

"We'll have to crawl for a while, then the tunnel will get bigger," Beren said.

For the next half hour, they crept along the dank, musty tunnel. The flickering lights threw fantastic shadows on the wall.

Sarah was right behind Josh, who followed Beren. She had always been afraid of going underground. Once, back in Oldworld, she had refused to go down into Mammoth Cave. Now, she said, all she could think of was worms!

Josh was having somewhat the same difficulty. He

held his torch as high as he could and gave a nervous start from time to time as the wavering light revealed a hole.

"Things will be a little better up ahead," Beren said, "but also it's a favorite hunting ground for the worms. Be careful!"

Suddenly the tunnel opened up so that they could stand. They still had to stoop over, and Volka could only go forward on his hands and knees, but it was better than it had been.

They had not gone far when Beren cried, "Watch out! Worms! They're crawling out of their holes!"

Josh had bad dreams for some time about what he saw next.

The torches threw their feeble light ahead, casting enough illumination so that he could see the holes along the sides of the cavern. At one of the openings a frightful sight appeared—a horrible head with bulging eyes and two spiked horns.

Behind Josh, Sarah choked back a scream. What came out of the hole looked like an enormous snake. And he knew that snakes were Sarah's second greatest fear, after being underground.

His own knees grew weak, and his hands trembled, but Josh hung onto the torch and his short sword tightly.

Beren, at the head of the group, was quickly joined by Josh, Dave, and Reb, all gripping swords.

"They'll strike like a snake!" Beren cried out. "Let them run themselves onto your swords."

Josh was appalled by the sight of the wormy creatures. First one or two emerged, then the whole cavern floor was filled with them. As they drew closer, the worms reared up like cobras, reddish eyes glaring. They had teeth, these worms, white and sharp. Josh well knew that teeth like that were only useful to carnivores—beasts that ate their prey.

He wanted to turn and run, but there was no place to run to. A worm reared in front of him, red eyes ablaze, and he could see drops of liquid on its needle-sharp horns. He held his sword high.

The worm drew back, then lunged. Josh felt the jolt as his sword caught the head of the monster. It drove him back a step, and the sword was nearly wrenched from his hand. But he held on, and the worm writhed fiercely, then grew limp.

"That's the way, Josh! Let them kill themselves!" Beren cried.

Reb was hollering loudly, and the others were shouting too. Some were crying, "For Goél! For Goél!"

The battle seemed endless. The Sleepers and their friends were driven back by the weight of the awful, squirming serpents. Dave performed heroically. He was the best swordsman and stayed in the forefront of the battle.

"Be careful, Dave!" Sarah cried out.

And even as she did, a worm came at him from the side, thrust forward, and caught him on the right forearm with one of its horns.

Dave cried out, and Reb leaped forward to pierce the head of the monster with his sword.

Dave blinked, gripped his arm, and then weakness seemed to come over him. Josh watched him fall into unconsciousness.

But Volka, the giant, seemed invincible. He picked up boulders that an ordinary man could not lift and sent them into the mass of worms, crushing them. He kept crying, "*Hroom, Hroom!*"—his favorite battle cry.

And then Beren cried out, "Look! They're leaving. We won!"

And that was the last of the battle. The worms were driven back into their holes.

Josh leaped over the worm carcasses and knelt beside Dave. At once Sarah joined him, crying, "Dave! Dave!"

Beren came too. He pulled back the sleeve of Dave's shirt and saw the wound. He shook his head gravely. "We'll do what we can." He leaped to where he had left his pouch and pulled a small leather bag out of it. "We'll have to draw that poison out," he said.

The Sleepers watched as Beren took out what looked like a rubber bulb. He attached it to Dave's arm over the wound and began squeezing it. "I hope it's not too late. The poison works very quickly."

"He—he looks like he's dying," Sarah whispered. She reached out and gripped Beren's arm. "Don't let him die," she begged.

"We need to get him out of here," Beren said. "Some of you carry him while I pump the poison. I want to get away. Those worms could come back."

Volka said, "Me carry."

Fortunately the ceiling of the tunnel rose even farther, and the sides widened. They were able to walk easily now. Only Volka had to stoop slightly. He carried the still body of Dave, while Beren walked alongside doing what he could for the wounded young man.

"There's light up there," Josh said.

"Those are the light-bearing stones," Beren said. "We can put out the torches now."

They soon found themselves walking by the pale green light that illuminated the passageway. This passage was much easier. The floor was flat here, and there were no rocks to stumble over—and no worm holes.

"The worms don't usually come this far. We set traps for them," Beren said.

"How's Dave?" Jake asked, coming up to look into the pale face of the boy.

"He don't look good to me," Wash said. "Don't you have medicine for worm bite?"

"We do have one other thing that might possibly help. Put him down, Volka, and we'll try it." Beren plunged into his sack again and brought out a small glass vial. "Hold his head so he can swallow this."

When Volka held the boy upright, Beren removed the stopper, put the little flask to Dave's lips, and forced the medicine down.

Dave swallowed convulsively.

"That may help some," Beren said. "But we've got to get away from here. Sometimes the empress's guards patrol this area. Not often, but I'd hate to be caught after coming this far."

The party made their way, for what seemed hours, through a maze of tunnels. Sometimes the ceiling lowered, forcing them to stoop over, and Volka had difficulty squeezing through. At other times they passed through large natural caverns.

"These are sandstone, washed out by an underground river. They weren't made by us," Beren said. "Up ahead is the river."

"That's good. I'm thirsty," Jake said.

The large river cut across the tunnel path. It came out of a huge cavernlike space on the left, flowed across, and disappeared into the rock on the other side.

"Where does this thing go?" Josh asked curiously. "It's a big one."

"It comes out on the surface, miles from here. But we never advise trying to use it," Beren said.

"Why not?" Sarah asked quickly.

Beren appeared to be reluctant to say. "Well, there are some bad things in here."

"Bad things?" Josh demanded. "What sort of things?"

"Blood fish."

"Blood fish!" Josh echoed. "What are *they?*"

"They don't sound good," Reb said, staring at the water. "I hope they're not what I think they are."

"They are fierce predators," Beren said. "In your world you may not have them. But they tear any living thing to pieces and eat it. I saw a goat fall in once, and in a few minutes all that was left was a skeleton."

"That sounds like a piranha back in our world." Josh glanced at the water. "How do we get across then?"

"We'll have to swim."

"Well, how do we know those fish won't get *us?*" Wash asked, looking apprehensively at the dark water.

"We don't. We'll just have to take a chance. They're usually drawn to blood. Do any of you have any scratches or cuts?"

Several had scratches from the sharp rocks, so Beren took time to bind up all of those. Finally he took a deep breath. "Well, there is no way to go around this river. So let's go. Hold Dave up as high as you can, Volka. Can all of you swim?"

It turned out that all of the Sleepers could, although Beren said, "We can wade most of the way."

It would be a chilling adventure indeed. As Wash crept slowly into the ice-cold water, he told Reb, "I'd just as soon be at McDonald's eating a chocolate ice cream."

Reb nodded. "Me too."

Josh was a fiercely brave young man, but he knew that the idea of being devoured alive by vicious fish took all the courage everyone had. "Come on. We've got to do it," he said desperately.

As it turned out, the crossing was not difficult. The blood fish were not active, and Volka stood in the deep part, handing the others across so they didn't have to swim.

They reached the opposite bank, and Josh took a deep breath. "Well, I'm glad that's over," he said. Then he sat down beside Dave. He stared into his white face and said, "I don't think he's any better. He looks worse, as a matter of fact."

"Yes, he is," Beren said. He looked down the twisting cavernous road ahead and added, "We must go quickly to a friend."

"A doctor? Do you know of one?" Sarah asked.

Beren shook his head. "But I know of someone else who could help."

They rose, and the small procession made its way through the winding cave. Behind them, the river and the worms seemed to stir as the darkness closed in.

10

A Desperate Venture

After many twists and turns in the underground passageways, Beren finally led the Sleepers into a large cavern with a high ceiling. As soon as they entered, many of the inhabitants rushed forward to greet him.

"This is my mother," Beren said. "Mother, these are the Sleepers."

"My name is Laiona," the woman said. There was a graciousness about her, and even though she wore rags and her face was lined with care, the Sleepers immediately recognized nobility in her.

"Why, you'd be the true Empress of the Underworld!" Sarah exclaimed. "Isn't that right?"

Beren answered. "She is the *rightful* empress, but we have been in hiding ever since Fareena and Lothar overthrew our royal house and killed my father."

"You must be tired," Laiona said. "Come. You must eat something."

"Mother, we have one who has been wounded," Beren said. "We were attacked by the worms."

Laiona turned her eyes to where the giant Volka held the limp form of Dave. "Then come quickly," she said. "How long ago did this happen?"

The rightful empress listened to her son's report as they made their way to her own compartment and saw to it that Dave was laid on a cot. Placing a hand on his forehead, she studied him carefully and shook her head. "We will do what we can," she said simply.

Sarah and Josh and the other Sleepers were escorted to another part of the cave. Beren saw that they were fed and, as they were eating, said, "When you're rested, I will show you around our home."

Later he took them on a tour. It was not what they had expected. He had told them of some of the wonders of the palace, but what they saw was more like a coal mine.

"We found this old mine shaft when we fled," Beren said. "Those loyal to my family came with us, and we wait here until by some miracle we regain the kingdom." He looked around at the dismal mine trap and shrugged. "It's not what we're accustomed to, but we're grateful to be alive."

The Underlings, they quickly found out, were a cheerful, kindly people. Their homes were carved into the sides of the tunnel, and the Sleepers stopped at one, where Beren made introductions.

"This is our former Chief of State, Dokar," he said. He laid his hand affectionately on the old man's arm. "He chose to suffer exile with us rather than remain in power under the evil empress."

Dokar was a small man with the usual pale features of those who lived under the earth, but his eyes were bright and blue. He smiled at them. "You are welcome to the Underworld. Come into my humble abode."

When the Sleepers were inside, they discovered that Dokar and his family had hollowed out a large room in the solid rock. They had left raised platforms for sleeping purposes, and also the table and chairs rose out of the rock floor.

There was a fire built into one wall, and Josh asked, "What about the smoke from the fire?"

Dokar explained to him the system of vents that had been carved, allowing the smoke to clear out of his home. Then he said, "Here—you must try some of this." He poured a clear liquid out of a stone jug into cups and passed them around. "I hope you like it."

Reb, along with the others, tasted it and exclaimed, "Why, this tastes like Coke!"

"What is Coke?" Dokar asked. Then when it was explained, he said, "This is a brew we make ourselves. Some of the ingredients come from the surface. We have a system whereby we can bring in our little necessities —vegetables, occasionally fresh meat—down from the surface."

The Sleepers listened as Dokar finished describing the lives of the Underlings.

Josh whispered to Sarah, "This is a hard way to live, always trapped in a cave—it's like being in prison."

"I suppose it's not as hard for them as it would be for us," Sarah answered. She looked around and saw the ragged dress and the pitiful implements and shook her head. "But it's bad enough after having been an empress to be reduced to this. In fact, it's awful! We've got to do something."

"I don't know what," Josh mumbled. "It looks like a hard situation."

Soon Beren led the group out of Dokar's home, and they stopped by the empress's compartment.

When they entered, Jake exclaimed, "Why, look! Look at Dave!"

The boy was resting, but the deadly pallor was gone from his face. His cheeks seemed almost rosy, and he was breathing evenly.

"That's great!" Jake exclaimed. "You must be a good doctor."

Empress Laiona smiled graciously. "We have learned a little of how to treat diseases and injuries, and the young man is exceptionally strong. He will be all right in the morning. I have given him something to sleep."

"We're very grateful, Your Majesty," Josh said. "I was very worried about him."

Laiona sat down, and when they were seated she said, "I would like to explain what has happened in our kingdom. I don't know how much Beren has told you."

"Not very much, Mother. Go ahead."

"We were deceived by the sorceress named Fareena. She came to us like an angel of light." There was a sadness in the noble face of the true empress as she went on to explain how Fareena had come promising them many wonderful things.

"Most of all, she spoke well of Goél and claimed to be his servant. We here in the Underworld are cut off from most things on the surface. But we know that Goél is the hope of Nuworld."

"How did she gain power, Your Majesty?" Sarah inquired.

"She has strong powers, very strong," the empress said, her lips drawing into a tight line. "She is, as I say, a sorceress and able to do more than we thought. She stole away the hearts and the minds of many of our finest. Even those on the General Council. And when she was strong enough, she and her henchman Lothar drew their strength against us. We had no chance at all," she said evenly. "It was only through the help of Dokar that we were able to escape. And even so, Beren was taken captive for a while."

"Many of our people were slain," Beren added. "And for a long time Fareena and Lothar sought us. Even now they are determined to slay all who are of our family."

Looking at the Sleepers, Beren leaned forward, his eyes intent. "We have heard of the mighty deeds of the Seven Sleepers. That is why I came to enlist your aid."

"But Lothar got there first," Josh said grimly. "How, I wonder, did that happen?"

"The Empress of the Underworld is no fool," Laiona said. "She is in firm alliance with the Dark Lord. We know that now. She is determined to enslave people. It is my belief that she sent Lothar to bring you to this place to make you captives."

"What for?" Jake demanded.

"If she could sway your minds and turn you against Goél," the empress said, "you'd be a mighty weapon in the arsenal of the Dark Lord himself."

"We would never do that!" Wash exclaimed. "We know who the Dark Lord is, and we would never serve him."

The empress shook her head. "You think not, young man, but you do not know the power of the evil empress. The Dark Lord himself, I think, gives her some power that I cannot explain."

Reb said suddenly, "I know what it's like. When we were at Camelot, there was a sorceress there. I didn't know it at the time, but—" he hesitated "—she just stole my mind away. You remember, Wash?"

The black face of Wash grew almost tragic. "I sure do, Reb." He shook his head. "It was like she took you out and she came in."

"That's exactly right. And that is what has happened to your young woman Abbey," the empress said.

"You know about her?" Josh asked in astonishment.

"We have our spy system, and we know a great deal about the empress and Lothar."

"Can we get to her? We've got to save her!" Josh exclaimed. Now he leaned forward. "That's why we came —to help you and to free Abbey."

"I fear she's in a serious condition. We have an agent in her quarters. Her name is Luna. Right now she is in the good graces of the empress, but she is one of us."

"What about Abbey? What does Luna say about her?" Sarah asked.

"She is well physically, but her mind has been ensnared by the empress. What kind of young woman was she? Tell me all about her. Some minds," she added, "are more susceptible to the wiles of the sorceress than others."

She listened carefully as Sarah took it on herself to describe Abbey. And when Sarah ended, she said, "She is exactly the sort that would be most easily swayed. I fear you would not know her if you saw her now."

"Abbey wouldn't do anything *bad*," Reb maintained stoutly.

"Not on her own, but you must remember your own experience, young man."

Reb's face fell, and Empress Fareena said in a kindly fashion, "We will hope for the best."

"What can we do?" Josh asked. "We'll try anything."

Beren said, "I have a plan. It's risky, but we must try something."

Beren had led the Sleepers down many corridors, some of them almost impassable. Volka groaned as he squeezed his enormous bulk through some of the tight places. "This place not made for giants," he mumbled.

"It's not made for Gemini twins either!" Mat exclaimed. "No good will come of this. I feel like a gopher down in a hole!"

His cheerful other half, Tam, slapped him on the shoulder and grinned. His face was dark with the silt that had fallen on it, but his teeth gleamed brightly. "Come now, brother!" he exclaimed. "We've seen darker things than this. We'll see some light down at the end of this tunnel."

"You'd be cheerful if the world was coming apart and the sun was falling," Mat grumbled. "I don't care what you say. Here we are, just a handful against a whole army—and a powerful sorceress besides."

The two argued on, and finally Beren turned and said, "You must be quiet now. We must not be caught."

"How are we going to get into Abbey's room?" Jake wondered. "We can't just go waltzing into the palace. There's bound to be guards."

"You're right, Jake. There are many guards." Beren's face was serious. "But there is a passageway that leads directly to the room where Abbey is kept. As a matter of fact, it was my room when I was growing up." He smiled briefly. "My mother the empress does not know everything. Behind one of the pictures in that room there is a hidden passage. I used to sneak out when I was a child. It was made a long time ago. No one knows when exactly. Even my parents did not know of it."

"They may have found it by now," Josh said.

"That may be. That's just a chance we have to take. But perhaps we can get into Abbey's room that way and bring her out. Come quickly now."

As quietly as they could, the Sleepers, accompanied by Volka, Tam, and Mat, made their way through an ever-narrowing corridor. Finally they came to a wooden door.

Holding his torch high, Beren whispered, "This is it. On the other side is the bedroom, part of the royal suite. Your friend is there."

Handing the torch to Jake, he drew open the door, listened a moment, and then slowly pushed at what appeared to be the back of a large frame. It swung aside, and suddenly the dark cave was illuminated.

Josh was standing right behind Beren. The light hurt his eyes at first, but after he blinked he saw Abbey!

Shoving by Beren, he stepped down into the room. He hardly noticed the richness of the jewels or the walls or the silks but called out eagerly, "Abbey!"

She had been dozing on a couch. Her eyes flew open. For an instant she looked unbelieving. Then she saw Josh and came to her feet. As the others came in, she called their names. "Josh—Sarah—"

Each one of them came to her, even Volka and Mat and Tam.

"How did you get in here?" Abbey exclaimed, staring at the opened tunnel. Then she stared at Beren. "Why, I remember you! You attacked me back at the camp."

"No, my lady. I did not attack you," Beren said. "I tried to save you."

Abbey listened as Josh tried to explain how they had gotten there, but her mind seemed slow. She appeared to be in a fog. She spoke slowly, not at all like her usual self. "Josh, and all of you, I have something to tell you. I have found the truth!"

Josh glanced at Sarah with alarm, then back at Abbey. "What do you mean, 'the truth'?"

"I mean," Abbey said, "we've been all wrong. Goél is not what we thought he was. We've been deceived."

The Sleepers listened with dismay as Abbey proceeded to tell how she had been as blind as they but now had learned that Fareena and Prince Lothar were their friends.

"We've got to join them," she said, speaking as one in a dream. "We must renounce Goél, and we must join the true people."

"You can't be serious!" Sarah cried. "What's wrong with you?"

"She's under the spell of Fareena," Beren said grimly. "We'll have to take her by force."

"Come with us. We have to save you," Josh said.

He took a step toward Abbey and was about to grip her arm, when suddenly she turned and ran across the room. She reached up and grasped a silken cord, her eyes wide. "I must save you from yourself!" She pulled the cord, and a gong sounded out in the corridor.

"We've got to get away from here," Beren said. He darted to the tunnel door, shouting, "Come!"

But the Sleepers could not leave Abbey. They gathered around her. Josh said, "We'll just have to take her."

At that moment the corridor door burst open, and suddenly the room was filled with soldiers. An officer spotted the tunnel opening and said, "They came in that way. Bar the door!"

Josh drew his sword, but instantly a half dozen blades were at his throat.

The officer shouted, "Throw down your weapons, or you will die!"

Josh saw there was no hope. He put his blade down. The others followed.

The officer smiled cruelly. "Take them to the retaining room, and I'll go inform the empress that we have captured the other six Sleepers."

11
Abbey Makes a Plea

I say execute them immediately!"

The empress was leaning back on a gold-encrusted throne, her eyes half-closed. Lifting her head, she glanced at Lothar standing before her, his lips drawn tightly together. "No," she said. "Once we do that, we cannot use them any longer."

"The Dark Lord would not agree." Lothar rarely argued with the empress, but now he had a determined look on his face. "You're well aware of how he has sent his agents all over Nuworld pursuing these Sleepers, and they had orders to kill them as soon as possible."

"Death is rather final." The empress smiled thinly. "We will try my plan first."

She had thought this thing over well. A fierce ambition burned in the breast of the empress. She saw being Empress of the Underworld only as a stepping-stone to greater powers. Now she said plainly, "There's an entire world out there, Lothar. We're stuck now in this hole of a kingdom; but if my plan succeeds, there is no limit to what we can do. Why, we'll be at the right hand of the Dark Lord himself."

Lothar looked doubtful. Shaking his head, he said, "It's a dangerous thing to tamper with his orders. You know what has happened to others."

The empress did not take well to opposition. She stood up and snapped, "I've told you what we're going to do. We'll try all of my powers to transform these children into servants of the Dark Lord. We have already succeeded with the girl. If we can bind their minds and transfer their loyalty from Goél to the Dark Lord, think what a mighty weapon it would be!"

Lothar stroked his chin thoughtfully. "That's true," he admitted. "But—"

"Enough!" the empress barked. "We will talk to the girl. She might be the one to help us."

They left the throne room and made their way down the corridor to the new quarters where they had moved Abbey after the secret passageway had been exposed.

Abbey's new room was far less ornate. She sat in one of two single chairs, waiting for the empress's customary visit.

She rose as Fareena and Lothar entered. "Oh, Your Majesty! I'm glad you've come!"

Fareena had a soothing note in her voice, saying almost in a whisper, "I'm sure you've been disturbed by the coming of your friends, Abbey."

"Oh, yes! We must do something to help them."

"That is exactly why I've come, my dear," Fareena said. "Now, you must not trouble yourself over this. We will find a way to help them, just as we have found a way to help you. Isn't that so, Prince Lothar?"

Lothar came over and stood beside Abbey. Placing his hands on her shoulders, he smiled down at her. "You must trust the empress completely, Abbey," he said. "We have found in the Kingdom of the Underworld that she is able to do that which others cannot. Trust her." Then he turned and left the room, giving the empress a significant look as he passed.

"Now sit down and let us talk," Fareena said.

When they were seated, Abbey began to express her dismay over the capture of the other Sleepers.

"I feel terrible," she moaned. "You don't know them like I do, Empress."

"That is true. You know them better than anyone else," Fareena agreed. "And for that reason, you are the one who must help them."

"I . . . help them? How can I help them?"

"By bringing them to the same knowledge of truth that you have found. They're still blinded by their loyalty to Goél, just as you were. But you have been brought to the light. Now you must help them."

Abbey's mind was filled with a host of confused thoughts. She loved her friends dearly, and the sight of them being carried away to the retaining room had stricken her. For some reason she felt that something was terribly wrong, and the words and tone of the empress did not help this time.

Fareena began her ritual. She lit the incense and slowly began her rhythmic chant. It took longer to be effective this time, for the girl's mind was struggling to break free. Still, after a long period, Abbey sat there, her eyes almost blank.

The empress said, "Now I will have you taken to your friends. Do your best to help them."

"Yes, I will, Your Majesty."

Fareena moved to the door, and a guard opened it. "Take her to the prisoners. When she's finished, bring her back to her quarters."

"Yes, Empress."

Abbey rose and followed the tall guard down the passageway. They moved to a lower level and finally stood before a steel door set in solid rock. It was guarded by no fewer than four soldiers. One of them, at the command of her attendant, opened the door, and Abbey stepped inside.

"Abbey!" Josh hurried to her.

Sarah took her hand. "I'm so glad to see you."

All the Sleepers gathered around. Volka took her other hand in his massive paw. As usual, Mat complained and Tam encouraged.

Finally Josh said, "What's wrong, Abbey? You look troubled."

"I've come to help you," Abbey said. Her lips scarcely moved as she spoke. She told them how she'd come out from her state of "blindness" and how she was now so happy to be the servant of the Empress of the Underworld. Her voice droned on, and there was a blank expression on her face.

The Sleepers stared at her aghast, then looked at each other.

Reb whispered to Wash, "That's not Abbey. That Empress has put her under a spell."

Wash shook his head. "She sure has. We've got to get her out of it."

Sarah had been instantly aware of the change in her friend. The two girls had become fast friends during their adventures in Nuworld, and now she took Abbey's hand again. "Come and sit down, Abbey. I need to talk to you."

Abbey obeyed and sat listening as Sarah spoke to her gently. But there was no break in the deadness of her voice or the frozen expression on her face. When Sarah tried to tell her that she was under the spell of the evil empress, she simply shook her head.

"No, the empress is my friend. She has helped me. You must all listen to her. She can help you."

For thirty minutes Sarah tried and then the others, but all to no avail.

At last Abbey said, "I must go back now. I would like to tell the empress that you are all forsaking Goél."

Josh gave a warning shake of his head to the others. "I wish you'd stay with us, Abbey."

"No, I must go back." She rose and went to the door. When it opened, she looked back, and for one moment there was a flicker of pain in her eyes, real human emotion. She started to speak—almost, it seemed, to cry out—but then somehow she could not. Turning, she left, and the door closed with a clang.

"Well, that's about as bad a scene as I want to go through," Jake said. "She's brainwashed. It's just like Abbey's not there anymore."

"We've got to do something to help her." Dave was sitting down, looking pale after his ordeal. He had a bandage on his arm, but otherwise seemed none the worse. "She's just like a dead girl."

They discussed Abbey for a long time.

"And this isn't the end of it," Josh said.

"You think they'll execute us?" Jake demanded.

"I guess if they were going to do that, they would've done it already," Josh answered. "What I think they'll do is try to hypnotize us like they have Abbey."

"Why are they trying to do all this?" Wash wondered.

Dave spoke up. "That's easy." He rubbed his wounded arm with his free hand. "You see, if we went out of here and attacked Goél's movement and stood for the Dark Lord, it would be a help to the Dark Lord. It would be confusing to those who have learned to trust us."

"We'll never do that," Josh said firmly. "But I want all of us to understand that what the empress has done to Abbey, she'll try to do to all of us."

"She'll never do it to me," Reb stated flatly. "I won't let her hypnotize me."

"Be careful about saying things like that, Reb," Josh said. "She's got strange powers. Any of us could become like Abbey."

"Oh, I couldn't stand that!" Sarah cried. "What can we do, Josh?"

He rubbed his chin thoughtfully. "I'm not an expert in this, but I think what we have to do is keep our minds fixed on who we are and who Goél is—and who the empress is. I think they've given Abbey some kind of drug, and there's nothing we can do about that. But when the empress talks to us, keep your minds off what she's saying. Think about Goél and what he's done for us and how he's saved us so many times. Think about the others in this group. Think how we're going to get out of this and how Goél is going to bring us to freedom again."

For a long time Josh and the others talked about how to combat the empress. Then he said, "That's all that we can do—don't let them break us down."

Josh's words were prophetic. Not half an hour after Abbey had left, the door opened, and a guard entered. He looked at Josh. "You! Come with me."

"Where are we going?" Josh asked.

"You have been sent for by the empress."

Josh looked over his shoulder, and Reb called out, "Don't give in, Josh. Remember Goél."

More than an hour later, as the Sleepers were pacing the floor, the door opened again.

When Josh walked in and the door clanged shut, Sarah ran to him. "Josh!" she cried. "Are you all right?"

There was a harried look in Josh's eyes, and his lips were tight. For a moment he didn't speak.

Sarah said, "Josh, can't you talk?"

When the words came, they came slowly. He said in a whisper, "Yes, I can talk. But that's about all."

"Sit down, Josh," she told him. She pushed him down onto one of the bunks, and his friends gathered around. "Tell us what happened."

Josh had difficulty speaking. There were breaks in his speech, and sometimes he would hesitate as if he had forgotten. He knew, however, that it was imperative that the others were prepared.

"They'll be coming for you—one at a time," he said. "The empress will try to put a spell on you. She'll . . . light some incense, and it makes you dizzy . . . your mind kind of slows down." He hesitated, while he collected his thoughts. "She'll talk to you. She's a good talker, real quiet and soft, and before you know it—" he looked around the group with anger in his eyes "—you find yourself *agreeing* with her."

"What does she want you to do?" Wash asked.

"She wants to turn us into beings like Abbey—to serve the Dark Lord. You've got to keep your mind on Goél and what he's done." He reached out to Sarah, and she took his hand. A small smile came to his lips. "All the time she was talking, I would think of what Goél's done for us since we came to Nuworld. As long as I could keep thinking of that, she didn't get me. But you can't let her take over your mind, or you'll be lost."

For a long time the Sleepers sat making plans.

Then another knock came at the door, and the armed guard stepped inside. This time he stood over Sarah. "You—the empress requires your attendance."

As Sarah went through the doorway, she paused for one moment and looked back at Josh. She smiled faintly and said, "I'll think about Goél." Then she left.

The door clanged, and there was a hollow sound in it that scared Josh.

"I hope we all can hold out," he said. "We've got to stay together."

"It looks pretty dark," Dave said. "We can't hold out forever. Time's on her side."

Wash, the smallest of them all, spoke up loudly. "Yes—but Goél is on our side." His brave spirit seemed to comfort the others.

Reb came over and patted him on the shoulder. "You've got a good attitude there, Wash," he said. "Now, let's get ourselves ready." A fierce light burned in his blue eyes. "You know, I'd like to put a spell on that old empress myself. Can't do that, but maybe I'll get a chance to whack her across the head with something."

Reb's fighting spirit brought cheer into the room, and they fell again to discussing strategy.

12
Beren Makes a Try

"It looks as if there is no hope." Dokar looked across at his young friend Beren. The two had been sitting for a long time in Dokar's cave, and hopelessness hung in the air.

Beren had told him how the Sleepers had been captured and how he himself had barely escaped.

Now Empress Laiona poured some liquid into a cup and said to Beren, "Drink this. You must be exhausted—and hungry too, I suppose."

"No, Mother, I couldn't eat anything." Beren's pale face bore the marks of discouragement. He took a sip from the cup, then shook his head. "They were the only hope we really had."

"It's not over yet," Laiona said. She sat down beside her son and for some time tried to encourage him.

Beren finally looked over at his mother. "You never give up, do you? I wish I had your spirit."

"You do have my spirit and your father's spirit too. I see him in you every day."

"What do you think he would've done if he were here now? I can't think of anything."

"I don't know what he would've done," Laiona said quietly. "But I know one thing—he would not have given up! We used to joke about it. He would say, 'I say I am firm, but your mother says I'm *stubborn.*'" She leaned back against the cold stone wall, thinking of days gone by, and her eyes grew soft. "I never knew your father to give up even one time. Sometimes things would get very difficult, and the rest of us would be depressed, but he would just stand there and say, 'We won't quit. Never give up.'"

"You speak the truth, My Empress," Dokar agreed. "He was a man who did not know the meaning of the word *quit*. As long as there was breath in his body, he would fight for what was right."

Beren listened as the two spoke of the old days when the family had been seated on the throne of the Underworld. It seemed long ago, almost like something he'd read about in a musty old book. He was exhausted, and failure had brought his spirits low.

However, for the rest of the morning he thought about what his mother had said. *Father wouldn't have stopped,* he said to himself many times. *But what can I do? We don't have enough power for an armed overthrow. What can I do?*

There seemed to be no answer. He went to bed that night asking, *What can I do?*

What followed then was a very strange occurrence. Beren was a heavy sleeper. It was almost a joke to his mother. "It would take an earthquake to wake you up," she often scolded. However, sometime during the night he suddenly came out of a deep sleep, fully awake. He sat up at once, put his feet on the floor, and reached for the sword that he kept beside him at all times. Fear came over him, which also was unusual.

"Who's there? Who are you?" he cried out.

"A friend."

Something in the voice that answered out of the stillness of the night seemed to calm Beren's fears. He stood, struck flint to a small candle, and made out a tall figure, wearing some sort of dark cloak, standing across the room.

"Who are you?" Beren repeated. "How did you get in here?"

"I can go where I please, as a rule." There was a touch of humor in the quiet voice and an absolute lack of threat that heartened Beren.

"I've come to encourage you."

Beren was so intrigued by this he almost forgot to demand again who the figure was. "Well, I need encouragement," he said. He took a step closer and squinted in the semidarkness. "I can't see you very well. Who are you?"

"I have many names. The name you will know best, perhaps, is Goél."

"Goél!"

Beren, of course, had heard of this mystical figure. The Sleepers had told him many tales of the strength and power and goodness of Goél. He could not speak for a moment. Then he said, "I'm so glad you've come, Goél. Your servants the Sleepers—they're in terrible danger."

"Yes, I know."

"Can't you do something?"

"I am doing something, my son." Goél hesitated. "The Sleepers must have told you that, as a rule, I do not intervene directly in the ventures of those who serve me."

"But you could just get them free. You're stronger than Fareena or Lothar—I know that."

"Most of my work is done through my servants," Goél said. "And that is why I've come. I ask you plainly, Beren, will you serve me?"

Beren had never seen Goél in his life. At times, he had even doubted his existence. The coming of the Sleepers had changed that, and he had been drawn to the stories they told. Now he was drawn to Goél himself. He said slowly, "I would like to serve you, but what can I do?"

Goél said, "When one comes after me, he must obey me—blindly at times. Are you willing to do this? To obey without knowing why? Even when the action seems desperate and foolish? Think well before you answer."

Beren was a very independent young man. To obey blindly was not in his nature. Somehow he knew he'd come to a crossroad—that he must either choose Goél or reject him forever. And he hated to give up his right to do what he pleased.

But standing in the dimness as the flickering light cast shadows over the tall figure, he had a glimpse of the chiseled face, the steady eyes, and the firm mouth, and he knew he had found the one he must follow. "Yes, Sire. I will obey. As best I can, I will serve you."

"Spoken like a true man and good servant!" Goél cried. He came and put his hand on the young man's shoulder. "You will have some dangerous times ahead. Never forget this moment when you decided to follow me. Now I must give you your first command."

Beren listened carefully as Goél spoke quietly. He said not a word during that time, and finally Goél said, "That is what I will have you do. Are you willing?"

"Yes. I do not see how it can be done, but I will do my best."

Goél smiled. "That is all I demand from anyone. Now go to sleep. You will need a good rest for your task."

Beren lay down, thinking he would not sleep a wink. He was so excited. But somehow his eyes were heavy, and even as he looked up from the bunk he saw that the cell was empty. A thought came to him, *This is all a dream. I haven't really been talking to Goél.*

But as sleep rushed in upon him, he said, "Dream or not, he's given me a plan, and I'm going to follow it."

The next morning at breakfast, Laiona saw at once that something was different about her son. His eyes were bright, and he moved with a certainty that he had been lacking. Looking across the table at him, she asked, "What has happened to you, Beren?"

Beren looked up from the food on his plate, which he had been eating heartily. A smile came to his lips, and he put down his fork. "You're probably going to think I'm crazy, Mother, but I've got something to tell you."

He grew excited again as he spoke of his visit with Goél, and his mother listened quietly, her eyes never leaving his face.

He said, "I told myself that it was just a dream. But I *know* that Goél was in my room last night, and I'm going to do what he told me."

"And what is that, my son?"

"He told me that I must go to the girl—to Abbey— and tell her the truth. She needs a shock, Goél says, to bring her out from under the spell of Empress Fareena."

"That will be very dangerous," Laiona said. "They know that you are on the loose. And she will be well guarded."

"I know that, but I promised Goél. I must do it." Then he said evenly, "I promised to serve Goél the rest of my life. I hope that does not trouble you, Mother."

The regal face of the true empress softened. "No, my son. For I am convinced that Goél is the power that will redeem this world. I myself will serve him—and all of our people. I know that he will not fail us. Only—be careful."

"I will be as careful as I can."

Shortly afterward, Beren bade his mother good-bye. He had strapped his sword to his side, adding a dagger in a sheath at his belt. In his hand he took a short staff. He carried a knapsack with food and a water bottle on a thong.

He left the village that was carved in stone and made his way down the dark caverns. It was a winding way, and he was alert lest he encounter any of the servants or guards of the empress. He knew soldiers were everywhere looking for him and that he would have no trial if he were caught. Fortunately he also knew the Kingdom of the Underworld as well as he knew his own hand.

For two days, he dodged through the tunnels, caverns, and holes that went down into the interior of the earth. Twice he was almost apprehended by Fareena's soldiers, only escaping by a hair's breadth.

On the morning of the third day, Beren found himself inside the palace, the most dangerous place of all. But he had grown up in this place and knew every inch of it. Only he could achieve this mission.

Servants were moving constantly about; soldiers and armed guards marched down the halls and were set at strategic points. Like a shadow, Beren slipped from room to hall to cavern. There were many secret passageways, and he used them all to best advantage.

Finally, by listening to the talk of the soldiers as he lay hidden, he discovered the room where Abigail was now kept.

He made his way there and saw an armed guard outside her door. "I can't get by him," Beren muttered. "I'll have to wait for a break."

Time crawled on, and Beren grew impatient. But at last the guard was changed, and the new man seemed less watchful than the first. As the hours crept on, Beren watched him grow sleepy. Then the soldier sat down in a chair, and his head slowly began to droop.

Beren waited until the man was motionless, then slowly stepped out of his hiding place. He crept past the guard, reached out, and took the door handle. Turning it, he slipped inside and closed the door silently.

Abbey was asleep on the bed.

"Abbey! Wake up. It's Beren."

Abbey came out of a fitful sleep and cried aloud when she saw him.

He held up his hands. "Do not be afraid. I will not harm you."

"What do you want?" she said. She remembered Beren, and it was in her mind that he was the enemy of Lothar.

"I want you to see something," Beren said.

"See what?" she asked in confusion.

"It will be very dangerous," he said. "And we must be very quiet. Will you go with me?"

Abbey had two impulses. One was to cry out for the guard, but something in the face of this young man prevented that. He looked so honest—and she *was* curious. She said, "I will go."

"I'll turn my back while you dress," he said. "Be quick."

Swiftly Abbey dressed, and together they slipped through the door. The guard, she saw, was sound asleep, and Beren led her down the hallway. Soon she found herself in a dark passage.

"I've known all these since I was a child," Beren whispered. "When my father was the king. Come. We must be quick."

He led her down many corridors, through many doors. Then he said, "We'll now go down to the lower levels."

A vague memory came to Abbey. She said slowly, "I've been there once—I think. Are we going all the way to the bottom?"

"All the way to the deep mines."

Abbey followed, and soon they were in such darkness as she never imagined. Only flickering torches broke it from time to time. "What is it that you want me to see?"

"I want you to see what has happened to our people because of Fareena."

Abbey, then, had a clearer memory. "I have seen some of it. I've seen women chained and forced to chip away at solid stone."

"That is what you must see again."

Beren took her to the lower parts of the deepest mine.

Abbey would never forget what she saw. Those who worked here were chained and almost skeletons. They barely had strength enough to raise the picks that they used to chip away at the rock. The guards were cruel; even children were treated viciously and slapped aside when they begged for food or drink.

"I don't want to see this," Abbey said. "Take me up."

"You *must* see it, Abbey. This is the truth about Fareena and Lothar." Then he took her arms and looked into her eyes. "You have been deceived by the empress—the diamonds and jewels are beautiful, but they're not the real thing. Look at that poor woman over there with those two children. They won't live long. They never do in the deep mines."

At a distance Abbey stood staring at the beaten forms and the guards who watched them like hawks.

Finally Beren said, "Abbey, suppose you were that woman. Think what it would be like to never know a kindness, to be starved, and to see your children starved. Is that what you want?"

"No!" Abbey seemed to be coming to herself. She said, "No, I never wanted anything like this." Somehow the sight of the slaves being so cruelly treated had blasted her loose from the power of the empress. She took a deep breath and looked up at Beren. "How could I have been so blind?"

"The empress has power to do that." He smiled. "Now you seem all right. How do you feel?"

Abbey shook herself. She took a deep breath and expelled it, saying, "I feel like I've been in jail somewhere, and now I can think and see how awful I've been."

"Can you remember all that happened?"

"I remember the rest of the Sleepers. They're trapped. Oh, Beren! We must get them loose."

"We will," he said. "Now that you're all right, you can see things clearly. Let us go."

"Where are we going?"

"I must get you back to your room. Then we'll make a plan."

They found their way back up, stumbling through the darkness, till finally they returned to the palace. When they reached the corridor where Abbey's room was, Beren peered cautiously ahead to see the guard standing. "He's awake now," he whispered. "We'll have to find some other way to get you inside. They mustn't know you've been gone, and they mustn't know you are yourself again. You'll have to pretend still to be a follower of Fareena."

"That'll be hard."

"You must do it," Beren insisted. "And I'll have to draw the guard away. I'll go out so that he sees me and follows me. When he's gone, you slip into your room."

"That's too dangerous for you."

"We'll have to do it. Quick now." Beren stepped out and allowed the guard to see him. The soldier let out a cry and ran toward him. Beren dodged away, and as soon as the two were pounding down the hall, Abbey raced to her door.

She opened it and slipped inside—and then she gasped, for Lothar and the empress stood in her room, staring at her.

"Had a little vacation?" Lothar asked coldly.

"I—I don't know what you mean," Abbey said.

The empress came forward and stared into her eyes. "She's out from under the spell," she snapped to Lothar. "I can't do it again. She'll have to be put with the others."

Even as she spoke, there was a scuffle outside. The door burst open, and when Abbey turned she saw Beren, firmly grasped by two large soldiers. He had been stripped of his weapons, and despair was in his face.

Fareena smiled, however. "Now, what have we here?"

Lothar grinned. "It seems we have the ex-prince. We've looked for him for a long time, Empress."

"Yes, I think we have them all now—the Sleepers *and* the prince."

Lothar said, "This time it will be my way, will it not, Empress?"

Fareena nodded. "Yes, I've had no success with any of them. They're all stubborn as beasts." She turned to the guards. "Throw these two in with the others. We'll deal with them later."

As they started to leave the room, Abbey drew herself up. "You'll not have your way with me anymore. I see what you are now. You're a tyrant and cruel."

"You challenge me?" Rage poured out of Fareena's eyes, and she took Abbey's face firmly by the chin, smiling cruelly. "You're very proud of your beauty. I saw that at once."

Abbey sputtered, "I-I-I was once, but I'll never serve you."

The empress drew a small knife with a jewel-encrusted blade from beneath her clothing. "Hold her fast," she told the guards.

At once Abbey was held in iron hands.

Still gripping the girl's chin, the empress placed the cold blade on her cheek. "If I slice your cheek, it'll make a terrible scar. Then you won't be beautiful anymore, will you?" She smiled as Abbey's eyes grew blank with terror. "Perhaps you have a choice to make. You'll either help me, or I will scar your face so terribly that no one will find you beautiful ever again."

She laughed aloud at the panic in Abbey's eyes. "I see that frightened you. Think about it then. You can have your beauty and serve me, or not serve me and be scarred for life. Which will it be? Take her away!"

Abbey was pulled away by the guards, and as she and Beren were hurried down the hall, Beren said, "Don't give up, Abbey. We still have Goél on our side."

13

A Crazy Dream

In the retaining room, the Sleepers surrounded Beren and Abbey.

As soon as Sarah looked at the girl, she cried, "You're all right again! Look, look at her eyes!"

Josh crowded close and saw that indeed Abbey's eyes were clear. "You're right," he exclaimed. He reached out and took both of Abbey's hands, saying, "Welcome home."

Abbey looked around, and tears came into her eyes. "I'm sorry that I said such awful things. I don't know what got into me."

"Never mind all that!" Reb cried. He gave Abbey a squeeze, wrapping his long arms around her. "You're back, and that's all that counts. Makes me want to give a Rebel yell!"

The others greeted Abbey warmly too, but then Beren said, "I know you're glad to have your friend back. Very rarely can anyone escape the coils of the empress."

"But what are you *doing* here?" Dave asked. "How did you get captured? What have you been up to?"

Beren began explaining how he'd had a visit from Goél, and immediately all the Sleepers were excited.

"Well, if Goél's on the job," Wash said grinning, his white teeth shining against his black face, "then we're all right."

"Well, not exactly all right *yet,*" Josh said, looking around. "We're still in prison."

"Aw, we've been in jail before," said Reb.

"Well, we haven't been in a jail quite as far underground as this one," Dave murmured. "Anybody got any ideas?"

"Yeah, Beren. You know this place," Josh urged. "Is there any way out of here?"

Beren leaned against the wall, tapped it. "Solid stone. Can't dig out through there." He looked through the barred steel door and said thoughtfully, "They've got enough guards out there to stop us. To tell the truth, I just don't know what to think."

"Well, we'll think of something," Josh said.

He tried to sound cheerful, but later he drew Sarah off to one side. She was the one he always chose to share his thoughts with. He'd learned he could say what he wanted to her—even confess that he was afraid.

He said as much now as they sat whispering. "You know, I'm trying to put on a pretty good act, but how in the world we're going to get out of here, I don't know."

Sarah took his hand. It was a natural action, and she smiled at him. "I can remember a time when you wouldn't admit being afraid."

Josh grinned. "That's what having a friend is—having somebody you can tell that you're afraid. I never thought you'd be the one. The first time I met you, I wouldn't have said that."

"You think about that time?"

"Sure do. I thought you were so pretty. The prettiest girl I'd ever seen, and I was so bashful all I could do was try to act tough."

"I thought you were awful," Sarah confessed. She giggled slightly. "I'd never seen a boy so puffed up with himself, or at least that's what it looked like."

"Good to have a friend, isn't it? Someone to tell everything to. Everybody ought to have at least one friend."

After a while a guard brought their food in a big black kettle with a wire handle and set it down. "Enjoy it." He grinned. "It might be your last meal."

When the door clanged shut, Sarah got up and began portioning out the food.

As Reb ate his, he said, "This is awful! What I wouldn't give for a mess of possum and greens!"

Abbey stared at him. "Well, *that* sounds awful!"

"Awful? There's nothing better than that," Reb protested. "Unless it's some pigs' feet or chitlins."

"What's chitlins?" Abbey asked.

"Don't ask," Wash said. "You don't want to know!" He took his plate and tasted his food. "Well, I guess it'll keep body and soul together. Sure would like a quarter pounder or a hot dog, though!"

After they'd eaten, Beren said, "I've got a feeling that if we're going to get out of here, it'd better be quick. I don't think Fareena had anything nice in store for us."

"As a matter of fact," Josh said, "you think she's going to execute us, don't you?"

"I think she will. She's been after me for a long time. Now it looks like we're all in the same boat."

They talked about various plans, none of them likely to succeed. The cell was gloomy and dank, and somehow the gloom communicated itself to all of them. Time passed slowly. There was no clock, no television, nothing to mark its passage. This seemed to make everyone even more depressed.

"If we were up on top, at least we could tell night from day," Jake protested. "Now I don't even know if it's midnight or high noon." Jake was ordinarily fairly optimistic, but he looked gloomy now and had no encouragement to give.

They never knew how much time passed. Food was brought but not regularly. Sometimes they'd grow very hungry; other times it seemed like only a couple of hours between meals. Hopelessness began to settle in on them.

Beren, strangely enough, was the most cheerful of them all. Perhaps he had had a harder life since his family had been deposed. But more than likely the reason was his recent visit with Goél.

Over and over he told the story of Goél's visit, and at first it cheered the others. After a while, though, he saw that they were growing more depressed, and discouragement began to get to him too. He began to think more and more that he'd just had a dream.

Time crawled on, and it looked as if the Seven Sleepers had reached the end of their career.

Jake pulled the ragged blanket around his shoulders, shivering against the clammy cold. Finally he dropped off to sleep, but it was not a sound sleep. It was filled with the dreams that had been coming to him lately.

Sometimes he'd dream that he was back at Disneyland in Oldworld, on one of the fantastic rides there. Other times he seemed to be in Atlanta, watching the Braves play baseball. Those were the good dreams.

At other times, however, awful dreams would come. Sometimes he dreamed of the Snakepeople, who almost killed them when they'd first come to Nuworld. Sometimes he dreamed of the cave people and of the T-Rexes that had almost gobbled them up. Nightmarish dreams.

This time those dreams faded away finally, and he somehow thought he was lying in a pleasant field filled with flowers and grass. The sun was warm on his face. That dream was pleasant, and he lay there soaking it up, knowing it was a dream, longing to truly see the blue sky, to smell the freshly plowed earth. To get out of this hole where he was buried alive.

He stirred restlessly, and another dream came to him. This was not like any of the others. He could not make heads or tails of it. Finally it passed, and he continued to sleep fitfully.

But the dream came again, exactly the same. Three times that happened, and then he woke up with a start.

Some of the others were awake and moving around, and Jake sat up and rubbed his eyes with his knuckles. "Wow!" he exclaimed. "What a crazy thing!"

"What is it? You been having bad dreams?" Wash asked.

"Sure have. Bad ones and good ones and one real lulu." He screwed up his face in thought and went over to get a drink of water. It was tepid and rank, but he drank it anyway. Then he turned and said, "That was a nutty dream. I wonder why I dream things that don't make any sense?"

Josh was bored out of his skull with the silence and with the monotony of their imprisonment. "OK, tell us about it," he said.

"First let me tell you about some of the others." Jake quickly told them about his earlier dreams, then shook his head. "Those make a little sense—those I've dreamed before. But that last one—and I dreamed it three times."

"You dreamed it three times? The same dream?" Beren said.

"Yes. What about it?"

"Among our people, we believe that such a dream has meaning."

"Well, this one doesn't make any sense. But I did dream it three times—exactly the same, every time."

"Tell it," Beren insisted. He leaned forward. "Maybe it does mean something."

Jake shrugged. "Well, I'll tell you about it, but it doesn't make any sense. It was real short, didn't last any

127

time. The first thing I saw was a table. Just a table sitting there, and I was looking at it. It looked like that one right there."

Jake motioned toward the single table that occupied the center of the room. "And it was a crazy thing. It seemed to turn into a door, and it swung open, and I stepped inside . . . how many of you saw that movie *The Wizard of Oz?* Yeah, all of you saw it."

"*I* never saw it." Mat sniffed. "What is it?"

"Oh, it's about this girl that gets sucked up into a tornado and taken to a fantasyland somewhere. But the thing about it is that one minute she's in a black-and-white world and the next minute she steps out into a world of color, blue skies, and green grass. Everything's beautiful. And it happened in just a moment's time."

"That was my favorite part." Sarah sighed.

"So anyhow, the table seemed to turn into a door, and I went through it, and everything was filled with color."

Josh waited, then said, "Is that all?"

"That's all. Nutty, isn't it?"

"Maybe not," Beren mused. "Obviously the dream has something to do with a table. You say it looked like this one."

"Just like it. Four legs and a top. What can a table look like?" Jake protested.

Beren's face grew solemn. He walked over to the table, reached down, touched it.

The others grew quiet, watching him silently.

Beren turned to face them. "For some reason, I think this table has something to do with a way out of here."

"You mean, you think it's a real door?" Josh asked, excitement rising in his voice.

"I can't think of anything else the dream could mean. Let's examine every splinter of this table."

They spent a great deal of time touching the table, looking for something different about it, until Reb said in despair, "It looks like a plain old table to me. I can't see that it's any door."

Beren said, "I don't see anything different about it either." He dropped his head, stood there thoughtfully, and then suddenly said, "Let's move this table! Grab hold of it."

Volka reached over and with one hand plucked up the table as if it were made of balsa wood.

Beren fell to his knees. "Maybe," he said, "it's something *under* the table. Wait a minute!"

The others crowded around.

"What is it?" Josh dropped to his knees beside Beren. "What did you find?"

"Look at this!" Beren said with excitement. "There's a line here—on the floor. This floor isn't solid. Here—help clean some of this dust and dirt away."

They worked frantically for a moment, and slowly an outline appeared.

Beren looked up, his eyes gleaming. "You know what I think? I think this is a trapdoor. If we can get it open, it'll lead to one of the passageways, and we can get out of here."

"But there's no handle, and it's made of stone," Josh observed. He tried to get a grip with his fingernails. "I can't get hold of it."

They all tried, and finally Mat growled, "Fat lot of good a trapdoor'll do us if we can't get it open."

Tam said, "Wait—we've each got eating utensils! Everybody get out what you've got."

There was a scurry as all of them grabbed their knives and forks.

Then Tam said, "Let's all stick the tip of our knife

blades right in this crack. Maybe we can raise it up just a little bit."

"Right," Beren said. "If we can just break it loose, I think Volka could get it."

Each one thrust the tip of his knife into the fine crack, but nothing happened.

Then Dave cried, "I think I saw it move, though. Put in the forks too. And everybody pull up hard."

Everyone jammed both knives and forks into the crack. And sure enough, the stone moved a little.

Volka reached down and put the tips of his fingers on it. "More!" he boomed. *"More!"*

They all tried frantically, and Volka managed to grab hold of it. His mighty muscles bulged. And then the stone shifted upward! Volka picked it up and said, *"Hroom! Hroom!"*

Beren said, "Look! It *is* a passageway! Quick! They might come for us any moment, and they'll try to follow. I'll go first. I don't know this tunnel, but if there's a way out, I'll find it. Volka, you squeeze through last. When you get through, see if you can knock some rocks loose to block the passage." He dropped feet-first into the hole, and one by one the Sleepers scrambled after him.

It was a very small hole for Volka, and he grunted as he squeezed through. He dropped down with a thud into the tunnel beneath, then began pushing loose rocks under the trapdoor. His powerful muscles rippled, and he said, *"Hroom! Hroom!"* again and again.

As the Sleepers followed Beren, they came very quickly to a larger tunnel.

"I know where I am now," he said. "Come. We've got to gather my people together. It's time to fight."

Josh said slowly, "We've got to overcome the empress, but I don't think it will be a physical battle."

130

Beren said, "Maybe not. But it won't hurt to muster what strength we've got."

Sarah asked Josh as they walked along, "You think we can win?"

Josh said, "She has a lot of power, but there's strength in Goél—if we can just find a way to use it."

14
The Battle

It was well that the Sleepers had Beren for a leader. They would not have known what to do. The young prince was everywhere, summoning the Underlings.

"I never knew there were so many of them!" Josh exclaimed, wonder in his voice.

Sarah and Josh watched as Beren went through all the secret passages, sounding the alarm. Now the corridors were filled with men, armed mostly with only staffs but some with swords, spears, and knives.

"They don't look like they could fight much. They're all weak and pretty washed out," Reb observed.

His words were overheard by Empress Laiona, who turned to the tall young Texan. "My people are brave," she said. "We are outnumbered, and we do not have the arms of the enemy, but we have a heart for freedom. And the time has come that we have long waited for."

Beren organized his troops into small battalions. He gathered the leaders together. The Sleepers watched as he pointed to a map spread out on the ground, instructing each one where he was to strike.

"We are weak," Beren said. "But our cause is right, and we fight for our families and our kingdom. Are you with me?"

A shout went up.

Wash grinned. "If they fight as good as they can shout, then this thing might work all right." He turned to Reb, who was shifting from one foot to the other. "Sure would like to have my old .44 here. Or my .33. I guess I'd take care of that old Lothar."

"Well, we don't have any guns and not nearly enough other weapons," Mat grumbled. "But I guess we'll have to do it."

"That's the most cheerful thing I've ever heard you say, brother." Tam grinned and slapped his identical twin on the shoulder. "You can be captain now."

Beren called out, "It's time to go. Follow me. Sleepers, you and your people stay close."

The Sleepers scrambled after Beren and his small force. They went through the usual maze of tunnels and corridors carved out of the rock.

Suddenly Beren threw up a hand and whispered, "There're some guards ahead. I want to take them alive. They might know something."

Beren chose four of his men, and they crept silently down the darkened passage.

The soldiers seemed half asleep and were taken completely off guard. The Sleepers pressed forward to hear Beren interrogate them.

"Where is the empress? Where is Lothar?"

One guard was a smallish man, and his eyes were wide with fright. "I can't tell. They'll kill us."

Beren, Sarah was sure, had no intention of harming the man, but he said roughly, "Well, you've got your choice. *They'll* kill you if they catch you, or *I'll* kill you now for sure. Volka, pull this fellow's head off for me."

Volka grinned broadly and reached out. He grasped the guard with wide arms and encircled his head with his mighty fingers. "*Hroom!*" he shouted. "I love to pull head off foolish guard."

"No! Wait!" the guard screamed. "Wait! I'll tell."

"Be quick then," Beren said.

The guard could not answer quickly enough. "The empress and Lothar are in the council room."

"Who's with them? How many guards?" Beren shot questions at the frightened man and soon turned to say, "We're not likely to have a better chance. The council room is off to itself. It will be guarded, but we can break through, I think. It's our best chance." He glanced at the trembling guard. "Tie them all up. Quiet, man! You can keep your head."

After the guards were made secure, Beren led the group on down the tunnel. Stopping at a corridor, he said, "This leads right into the palace. When we get there, we'll have to take the guards out. We can't let any of them get away to get help. Are you ready?"

"I'm ready as rain," Reb said. He was holding a sword in his right hand and a club that he had picked up in his left. "Let's do it!"

Beren grinned. "I hereby appoint you sergeant. Come on, Reb."

The two young men burst down the corridor and were confronted at once by a rank of heavily armed guards. Reb let loose a screeching battle cry as steel clanged on steel.

Then the other Sleepers came boiling in and formed a line with Reb and Beren. The guards outnumbered them, but slowly the fury of the Underlings combined with that of the Sleepers proved too much. Gradually the guards were forced back, and finally the survivors threw down their weapons, crying for mercy.

"Tie them up too," Beren commanded. "Now we have a chance. Come, you Sleepers. To the council room!"

Beren charged through the door followed by the Sleepers. Inside the large room, dominated by a huge table and large chair at one end, sat Lothar and Fareena, who rose at once. Three other men were in the room, members of the High Council.

"Throw down your weapon, Lothar!" Beren cried out.

Lothar, instead, pulled his sword and bore down on Beren. "I will put you in your place once and for all."

The Sleepers started to surround Beren, but the prince cried out, "No! Let me handle him." He advanced, and soon the two were engaged in a furious duel.

"What if Lothar kills him?" Sarah gasped.

"That'll never happen," Josh answered. "Look, Beren's getting the best of him already."

The Sleepers watched nervously as Beren beat down the blade of the larger man. There was a skill in the young man that they had never seen before. The swords flashed, and the blades sang in the air. Then suddenly, the sword of Lothar was on the floor, and Beren's blade was at his throat.

"Don't kill me," Lothar cried, falling to his knees and holding up his hands in surrender.

"You've got him!" Josh shouted. "Keep him right there. The rest of you men stand still."

The Empress Fareena was watching with blazing eyes. Now, as every eye turned to her, she stood even taller. "You're fools to come into this room," she said. "My power here is at its greatest."

Beren said, "I fear you not, Fareena."

"Then you are a fool. You do not know the power of the Dark Lord, which he has given to me."

She lifted her hand high then and began to speak in a strange language. The room grew darker as though a fog had swept in. It was a darkness that almost had a body to it. Sarah thought each member of the Sleepers, as well as Beren and the Underlings, must be feeling a shiver of fear.

There was a smell of evil in the air, so thick that it seemed to weigh her down. Sarah almost fell to her knees, so heavy was the sense of wickedness.

The empress cried out, "You cannot resist me. You have stood against me and against the Dark Lord, and now you all will die."

"You will die first," Beren shouted. But for some reason he seemed to suddenly lose strength, and his sword dropped to the stone floor with a clatter.

The empress laughed, and Lothar rose to his feet with a grin of triumph on his cruel lips.

"Now," Fareena said, "we will see."

Beren cried out with hatred in his voice, "You are an evil being. I hate you with all my heart."

Several shouted out their loathing for the empress; and the more they cried, the darker the room seemed to grow.

Sarah was now almost smothered by the feeling of evil. She felt herself slipping into unconsciousness, and for one moment hatred for Fareena and all she stood for rose in her throat, almost choking her.

Then she heard a voice, a voice that sounded very familiar.

"Remember what I told you, my daughter? You can only overcome evil with good. Never with a sword."

At once Sarah stood to her feet and lifted her hands. "Listen to me," she said. "We must stop letting hate have its way."

The Sleepers looked at her. Beren also, although he was almost doubled over, turned to face her along with his lieutenant.

"That's her way—to hate," Sarah said. "That's what she's done to the world. We must not hate!"

"What then can we do?" Beren asked.

"Let them see what *love* is."

"I can't love her!" Abbey cried out. "Not after what she did to me!"

"Then love your friends, your brothers. Love Goél, love the good. But don't focus on hate."

Sarah found, even as she spoke of love, that her own hatred was somehow being vanquished. She looked over at Josh and remembered the many things they had done together, and she felt her love for him grow. She looked at Abbey, at Reb and Dave, at Jake and Wash, and remembered how close they were. Love rose in her, and she saw it rising in the others too.

Even as Sarah fixed her mind on love for others, the dark fog began to diminish.

The room grew lighter, and Reb cried out, "It's working! Shoot, I guess I can love as good as anybody."

Josh looked up at Fareena, whose face—pale already —seemed now bloodless. She clutched at her heart, and her lips twisted in what seemed to be agony. "Stop it!" she cried. "Stop it!"

And suddenly Sarah felt pity for her. "You've never known love, have you, Fareena? You've missed out on everything. I feel sorry for you."

Fareena screamed in rage and cried out to Lothar, standing again with sword in hand.

But Lothar saw that the empress's powers were fading. And as the victors began to shout, his eyes met those of Fareena. He seemed to understand an unspoken command, and with a cry he leaped toward Abbey, his blade flashing down.

Sarah saw him move, but it was too late. The sword ripped through Abbey's cheek, and she fell backward, uttering a moan.

Beren leaped forward, seizing his fallen sword and striking the weapon out of Lothar's hand. "I could kill you for that! But you'll have a fair trial. You and your evil mistress."

But Sarah was not thinking about Lothar. She was kneeling beside the still form of Abbey. When she saw the damage to Abbey's face, the terrible cut that was bleeding freely, she looked at Josh and said, "We've got to get her help. She's badly hurt."

"Yes, that's got to be sewed up," Josh said. He was barely aware that Beren was binding Fareena and Lothar. "We've got to get a doctor quickly."

Then Beren was at his side. "There will be a battle we must win now with the followers of Fareena—but we will get a doctor at once." He bent over and touched Abbey's hair and said quietly, "You were most brave, my dear Abbey. We will find help for you."

15

The Victory

After the capture of the empress and Lothar, the battle went swiftly. The servants of Fareena put up a stiff fight at first, but the Underlings, inspired by Beren, swarmed through the kingdom.

The Sleepers were in the midst of it, as usual. Several times, as usual also, Josh had to caution Reb, for the young Southerner was reckless.

"I just forget where I'm at when I'm in a fight," Reb said. "Especially a winning fight like this one."

Beren performed magnificently. He maneuvered his smaller army through hidden caverns and concealed passageways so that they poured in on the servants of the defeated Fareena unexpectedly.

And word got out to the entire kingdom that Beren of the Underworld was rising in revolt against Empress Fareena. From far under the earth the Underlings heard and responded.

The fight was not without loss—many Underlings were wounded and some of them killed—but at last Beren could say, "Come. Now we will free those in the deep mines."

He led the Sleepers and his small army downward to the mines. They fought their way through until finally the guards threw down their weapons, calling for mercy.

"Set all the slaves free," Beren cried out in a ringing voice.

The Sleepers found this to be the most enjoyable thing they had done in the Underworld. Each of them secured keys to fit the chains, and they moved among the slaves and set them free. Many times those who had been down in the mines for long years broke into tears.

When all were liberated, Beren said, "Now we leave these accursed mines."

"Who will do the mining now that there are no more slaves?" Josh asked.

Beren flashed him a grin. "I think we might find some volunteers among the servants of Fareena."

Dave nodded grimly. "Lothar might do well down here."

They climbed upward, and the ex-slaves began to sing. The sound of their singing reverberated through the caverns.

Later in the day, the Underlings and the Seven Sleepers and their friends gathered in the palace amphitheater for a special announcement. Empress Laiona was stepping down from the throne in order for Beren to rule the Kingdom of the Underworld.

All of the former slaves looked up to where Beren and his mother stood on a raised shelf of rock, and a great cry went up. "Three cheers for Beren the King!" and the amphitheater rang with glad voices.

Beren raised his hand for quiet. "You are all free now. There will be no more slavery."

After he had dismissed the people, he turned to the Sleepers. "Now we will show you what a real Underworld banquet is like."

It was a little later that the Sleepers, who had bathed and put on fresh clothing, came to the banquet room. All were there except Abbey, who was still being treated by the court physician.

"I'd rather stay with her," Sarah said to Josh.

"I know, but this is necessary. They want to honor us, and we have to give them the chance. Afterward, you and I will go sit by her."

The banquet room was bright with light and color. Music filled the hall as King Beren entered. All rose and lifted their toast. "To the King of the Underworld—King Beren!"

Beren flushed and ducked his head. "I'm not used to these new honors, but I will rule my people as well as I can." He seated his mother, and then they all sat down to eat.

And what a feast it was! The former royal cook had been released. He had raided the storehouse and prepared the best to be found. There were meats, breads, soups, even fish, caught in underground streams. Afterward there were unusual desserts that the Sleepers could not even name.

Then the king arose. "I propose a toast to the Seven Sleepers, the servants of Goél."

Everyone stood and lifted their glasses high.

When they were seated again, Josh said, "This all sounds good, but I'm worried about Abbey."

Beren said, "I, too, am worried. What does the physician say?"

"She will be badly scarred," Sarah said sadly.

"That is a tragedy." Beren shook his head. "But her scar will be a scar of honor."

"I suppose," Josh said. "Still, it's going to be hard for Abbey. I wish it had happened to me instead. I'm ugly enough already. One more little scar wouldn't have hurt."

"You are *not* ugly!" Sarah snapped. "But you're right about Abbey. She was always proud of her looks. I wish it hadn't happened."

Laiona had said little, but now she spoke. "Freedom never comes cheaply. Some of our people are dead; some have endured years of chains. But now it grieves me that this young girl, not one of our own, has paid such a terrible price for our freedom."

Jake said, "It's bad all right, but somehow I think she's going to be able to handle it."

"What makes you think so, Jake? You know how she always valued her beauty."

"I talked to her for a little bit just before we came here. She's quieter than she ever was, and there's something different about her."

"I think an experience like this helps make us who we are," Josh mused. "You know, there's an old saying—'It's better to go to the house of mourning, than it is to go to the house of feasting.'"

Reb lifted his head. "What's that mean? Are you saying it's better to go to a funeral than it is to go to a party?"

Josh nodded. "I guess there's something to that, Reb. Going to parties doesn't make us any better or any tougher or able to understand people any better. But hard times do. So in that sense I guess hard times really *are* better for us than good times. Although I'm not going out looking for them."

"We don't have to go out looking for them," Mat grumbled. "They just come." But he mellowed, for he was very fond of Abbey. "I, too, hate to see this come to Abbey. She's been spoiled, but underneath she's always been a sweet girl."

Finally the banquet was over, and Beren said, "We will go now and visit Abbey. Whatever the King of the Underworld may do will be done."

"Unless you can give her a new face, there's not much that can be done," Wash said sadly. Then he asked, "What's going to happen to Fareena and Lothar? You're not going to execute them, are you?"

"They deserve that, but we will show mercy," Beren said.

"Do you think there's any hope they can ever become other than what they are? They're so evil!" Sarah exclaimed.

"I have learned one thing," Laiona said quietly. When they looked at her, she smiled. "There's hope for everyone!"

16

A Badge of Honor

King Beren proclaimed a feast for seven days to cele-brate the freedom of all his people. During that time, the Sleepers toured some of the more wonderful parts of the Underground.

They discovered that far underneath even the deep mines there were wonders to be seen. Underground rivers so deep that they seemed to have no bottom were filled with unusual—and delicious—fish. They were taken on a long journey to where rich jewels could be plucked from the walls.

But Abbey was always on their minds, and especially on the heart of Beren. He went to her compartment one day to have a private word. He found her sitting with her scarred face turned to one side as if to hide it.

"Abbey." Beren took a seat in front of her and reached out for her hand. "I'm glad to see you doing so well."

"Thank you, Your Majesty."

Beren shook his head. "I could never be that to you. 'Beren' and 'Abbey' we will always be to each other." He stared at her for a moment, then released her hand. "I want to say something."

Abbey turned slightly to look at him, still keeping her wounded cheek turned away. "Yes, what is it, Beren?"

Beren hesitated, then said, "Why don't you stay here?"

"Here? In the Underground?"

"Yes. You could be a princess here. Have all the diamonds you want. You love them, don't you? Fine clothes —all will be yours. Anything you ask for."

An odd look came into Abbey's eyes. She paused for only one moment, then shook her head. "I don't seem to care much for things like that anymore."

"You don't?"

"No. And that's very strange because I always did, you know. I always wanted pretty clothes and fine stones and all kinds of luxury and ease."

"Well, I suppose most girls would like to have those," Beren said.

"No, it was not a healthy thing with me at all. I thought all the time about how I looked, even from the time I was a little girl. You don't know the hours I've spent fixing my hair and trying this and that to look better. I was so determined to be the prettiest girl at every party." She looked sad for a moment, then shook her head, and her blonde hair cascaded over her shoulder. "But it's not good for a girl to be like that. I've found out something."

"And what is that, my Abbey?"

"What Goél and others have tried to tell me for a long time." Now she did turn, and Beren saw the ugly scar coursing down her cheek. "I found out that it's not the outward beauty that counts but that which is inside."

Beren was taken by her words. He reached out and clasped her hand again. "Stay here with us. You will be honored. You will be Princess Abbey."

"No." She shook her head. "I must go with the others. Our work here is done."

When Beren left, Abbey walked over and looked at herself in the mirror. For a long time, she was absolutely still, then a tear appeared in one eye. She reached up quickly, wiped it away, and said, "None of that. You mustn't cry. Not ever."

Later, Sarah came to visit and spoke of their departure. But that seemed not to be what was on her heart. Finally Sarah said, "Abbey, can I talk with you?"

Abbey looked at her in surprise. "Of course. What is it, Sarah?"

"This is hard, but I want to know how you really feel about . . . about . . ."

At once Abbey touched the scar. "You mean about this?"

"Well . . . yes. About that."

"I wish it hadn't happened," Abbey said. "No one would want a thing like this." She lowered her hand, then sat looking down for a moment. When she lifted her eyes, there was a quietness about her that had not been in Abbey before she was wounded.

At last she said, "It's funny. I've always been the one the most conscious of appearance, and now I'm the one to lose it. But I can live with it, Sarah."

Sarah came over and put her arm around the girl and hugged her. "I'm glad you're looking at it like that. Your looks won't matter to anyone who loves you."

Abbey did not answer immediately but then said, "I'm afraid it will matter to some. Not everyone is kind like you and Josh and Reb and all the others."

Then the doctor came in. He examined the scar. He said, "I'm glad the blade didn't take your eye. That would've been terrible."

Abbey traced the scar tentatively with her fingertips. "Will it grow smaller as time goes by, Doctor?"

The doctor fidgeted. "Perhaps. But of course your cheek will never be as it was before this happened. You understand that, don't you?"

"I understand," Abbey said. "Thank you, Doctor."

After the physician and Sarah left, Abbey read for a while. She did not want to talk to anyone else just now, and the quiet was soothing. At last she blew out all the candles except one and lay down on her couch. It made a soft bed, and soon she fell asleep.

"Abbey—awake!"

At the sound of a familiar voice, Abbey opened her eyes, startled, and sat up. "Goél!" she cried out. "You're here!"

"Yes, I am here." Goél took her hands and pulled her to her feet. His hands were warm and strong, and as she looked up at him, she felt as if she wanted to cling to him and never let him leave her sight again.

"You have had a hard time."

"Yes, I have been very disobedient. I should never have let the Sleepers go without me. That was very wrong of me."

"I'm glad you recognize that." Goél nodded. He still stood before her quietly, holding her hands. "You are changed, my Abigail," he said gently. He released one hand and reached up to touch the scar on her face. "You have changed on the outside. This is a bad thing."

His sympathy caused tears to form in Abbey's eyes. Her throat was thick, and it was hard to answer. "I have changed inside too, Goél," she whispered.

"And how is that, my daughter?"

"I have learned—finally—what you wanted me to learn. That it is what is in the heart that counts, not what is on the outside."

Goél's hand remained on her cheek for a moment longer, then he lowered it. "Sit down. I must tell you some things."

For some time Goél spoke to her. His voice was quiet and soothing, and she felt secure. Then he stood. "When I first saw you, I knew there was a fine young woman in you. You were too concerned with your beauty, as I told you, but now you have learned the way of Goél. I am proud of you, Abigail."

He turned then and left the room.

Abbey sat down weakly, her knees feeling very unsteady. She thought of what he had said and went back to lie down. That night she dreamed of all that had taken place. But always she would remember his words, the kindness of his eyes, and the touch of his hand on her scar, and she smiled in her sleep.

Abbey rose at daylight and dressed quickly, then collected her things.

A servant announced, "It is time to leave, my lady."

"I'm coming." Fastening a cloak around her shoulders, she left the room. It did not occur to her that for once in her life she had not looked in a mirror to see if her hair was arranged properly.

When she came to where the other Sleepers had gathered, they were all prepared to leave.

Abbey said, "I'm ready."

Everyone stared at her.

She faltered. "What . . . what's wrong?"

Sarah came over, her lips trembling. She reached out and touched Abbey's face. She could only whisper, "Abbey, your scar—it's *gone!*"

Startled, Abbey touched her cheek, and a shock ran through her when she found it to be smooth and perfect. Her lips formed a name, and tears formed in her eyes.

"It was Goél, wasn't it?" Sarah asked, putting her arms around the girl.

"Yes. He came to me last night, and he touched me, but I didn't know—"

They all gathered around her then, and there was rejoicing among the Sleepers.

When Beren arrived, he could not believe his eyes.

"Now," he said, "you have it all back again and more besides."

After breakfast, Beren himself led the Sleepers through the caverns to the door to aboveground. It opened with a rustling sound, and as Josh stepped out into the sunlight, he let out a cry. "I've never seen anything so beautiful."

He looked at the blue sky and white clouds, the green grass, and the trees waving their branches in the breeze. "I'm glad to be back out here again."

Sarah asked, "Beren, don't you want to stay aboveground?"

"I will come up from time to time. But every man and every woman to his own place. The Underworld has its beauties too." He turned to Abbey and whispered, "Will you not stay and be Princess of the Underworld?"

Abbey smiled and took his hands firmly. "No, Your Majesty. I must go with the Sleepers. That is how it is with the servants of Goél."

There was sadness at the parting. Beren mounted them on fine horses, and as they rode away from the gate, some of that sadness remained.

"It's a nice place to visit, but I wouldn't want to live there," Jake said.

Sarah noticed that Dave and Abbey were riding very close together, and she smiled. Glancing across at Josh, she asked suddenly, "Would you like me just as well if I had a scar like Abbey had?"

Josh turned to her with surprise. "Why, I'd like you, Sarah, if you were as ugly as a pan of worms."

Sarah laughed aloud. "You have a way with words, Josh."

Reb was riding just behind them. "You know," he

said, "a cousin of mine left home and came back with a bride. And she was bad ugly!"

Josh never knew when the Southerner was teasing him. "Real ugly, was she?"

"They said she was so ugly when she was a baby, they had to tie a pork chop around her neck to get the dogs to play with her."

"That's pretty ugly." Sarah smiled. "How did her family take it—his bringing home such an ugly girl?"

"Oh, they didn't like it, of course." Reb shrugged. "But the groom, he said, 'Well, beauty's only skin deep, Pa.' You know what his pa said?"

"What'd he say, Reb?"

"He said, 'You'd better skin her then!'"

A laugh went up around the Sleepers who had been listening to this.

Josh said, "Let's get to where we're going." He reached over and punched Sarah on the arm. "Don't worry. You're not going to get rid of me, no matter how homely you get."

The seven rode on, trailed by the giant and the two dwarfs. They were all happy to be out of the Underground, but it was Abbey who seemed happiest of all. She glanced at Dave, who was looking handsome as usual, and said, "I'm glad to be like I am, Dave."

"You look better than ever," Dave replied with admiration.

But Abigail Roberts had learned better than to put overmuch value on looks. She said, "I mean I'm glad to be alive and healthy—and I'm glad to have friends like you, Dave. Come on. Let's go see what Goél has in store for us now."

Get swept away in the many Gilbert Morris Adventures available from Moody Press:

"Too Smart" Jones
4025-8 Pool Part Thief
4026-6 Buried Jewels
4027-4 Disappearing Dogs
4028-2 Dangerous Woman
4029-0 Stranger in the Cave
4030-4 Cat's Secret
4031-2 Stolen Bicycle
4032-0 Wilderness Mystery

Come along for the adventures and mysteries Juliet "Too Smart" Jones always manages to find. She and her other homeschool friends solve these great adventures and learn biblical truths along the way. Ages 9-14

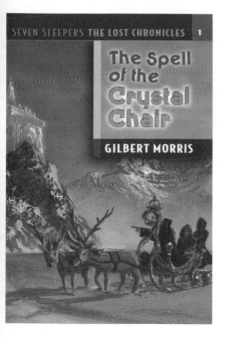

**Seven Sleepers -
The Lost Chronicles**

3667-6 The Spell of the Crystal Chair
3668-4 The Savage Game of Lord Zarak
3669-2 The Strange Creatures of Dr. Korbo
3670-6 City of the Cyborgs

More exciting adventures from the Seven Sleepers. As these exciting young people attempt to faithfully follow Goel, they learn important moral and spiritual lessons. Come along with them as they encounter danger, intrigue, and mystery. Ages 10-14

Dixie Morris Animal Adventures

3363-4 Dixie and Jumbo
3364-2 Dixie and Stripes
3365-0 Dixie and Dolly
3366-9 Dixie and Sandy
3367-7 Dixie and Ivan
3368-5 Dixie and Bandit
3369-3 Dixie and Champ
3370-7 Dixie and Perry
3371-5 Dixie and Blizzard
3382-3 Dixie and Flash

Follow the exciting adventures of this animal lover as she learns more of God and His character through her many adventures underneath the Big Top. Ages 9-14

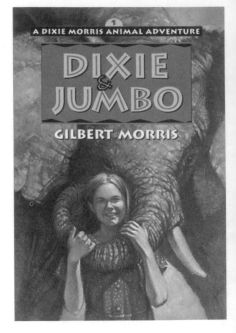

The Daystar Voyages

4102-X Secret of the Planet Makon
4106-8 Wizards of the Galaxy
4107-6 Escape From the Red Comet
4108-4 Dark Spell Over Morlandria
4109-2 Revenge of the Space Pirates
4110-6 Invasion of the Killer Locusts
4111-4 Dangers of the Rainbow Nebula
4112-2 The Frozen Space Pilot

Join the crew of the Daystar as they traverse the wide expanse of space. Adventure and danger abound, but they learn time and again that God is truly the Master of the Universe. Ages 10-14

Seven Sleepers Series

3681-1 Flight of the Eagles
3682-X The Gates of Neptune
3683-3 The Swords of Camelot
3684-6 The Caves That Time Forgot
3685-4 Winged Riders of the Desert
3686-2 Empress of the Underworld
3687-0 Voyage of the Dolphin
3691-9 Attack of the Amazons
3692-7 Escape with the Dream Maker
3693-5 The Final Kingdom

Go with Josh and his friends as they are sent by Goel, their spiritual leader, on dangerous and challenging voyages to conquer the forces of darkness in the new world. Ages 10-14

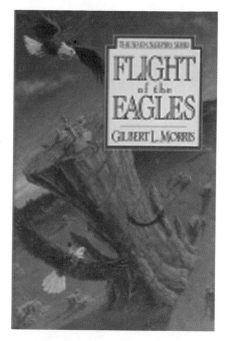

Bonnets and Bugles Series

0911-3 Drummer Boy at Bull Run
0912-1 Yankee Bells in Dixie
0913-X The Secret of Richmond Manor
0914-8 The Soldier Boy's Discovery
0915-6 Blockade Runner
0916-4 The Gallant Boys of Gettysburg
0917-2 The Battle of Lookout Mountain
0918-0 Encounter at Cold Harbor
0919-9 Fire Over Atlanta
0920-2 Bring the Boys Home

Follow good friends Leah Carter and Jeff Majors as they experience danger, intrigue, compassion, and love in these civil war adventures. Ages 10-14